City of Roses

by Donovan Pruitt

City of Roses is a work of fiction. Names, characters, businesses, places, events, and incidents are either the products of the author's imagination or used in a fictitious manner. Any resemblance to actual persons, living or dead, or actual events is purely coincidental.

ISBN: 978-1-943352-00-5

Cover Design by: Damonza

www.damonza.com

Edited & Formatted by: Michelle Josette

www.mjbookeditor.com

Published by Kala Empire Publishing, LLC

For those who remember.

For those who will never forget.

Chapter One

There had been a woman in his headlights. She was a blur on the road, a temporary streak of visual noise coated in a thin white veil that glimmered in the motorcycle high beam. Alex had done everything he could do to avoid her, much to his detriment. He could still hear the squeal of his skidding tires, the buzzing wail of their airborne spin toward the trees, and the hollow punch of his body into the earth.

The fire at his back urged him forward, but the haze of blindness from his fall beckoned the utmost caution. The Geiger counter flipped from his wrist, clicked, and instantly flashed red.

Images flooded his mind to stabilize his failing condition—a last-ditch attempt to stay anchored to consciousness. His body was cold with washes of stinging pain and targeted chills, likely from open wounds and fresh blood. Groaning, Alex crawled forward along the forest floor. Each crunching branch and shuffle of soil echoed out like an extension of his seemingly broken body. He didn't know where he was going, or in which direction, but he knew he had to escape the flames of the wreck in his wake.

Each blink wore heavy. The world disappeared for seconds at a time as his eyelids struggled to part. But even lacking clarity of vision, he knew what would happen if the flames found their way to the gas tank. His body heaved forward, struggling with his last ounce of strength to push along and advance to safety, as far away from the bike as his body would allow.

His ears deceived him. What began as a distant vehicular engine in the distance was replaced by the heavy drums of an encroaching gallop. Alex was more than surprised to hear horses coming to his rescue, but his relief was shortly soured by the heart-stopping growl that shook the very trees around him. A howl ripped through the night air, more fiercely horrible than any dog or wolf.

He could feel the beast's nostrils flaring as it sniffed, searching the area. It marched in a wide circle around him, claiming its prey. Alex panicked, but found himself physically unable to resist an assault. With his consciousness already drifting away, he succumbed to its call and closed his eyes, allowing fate to take its course.

*

When his eyes snapped open, it was unmistakably the sound of gunfire calling him back to life. Alex heard the stalking beast huff in defeat before turning and charging through the woods. Rifle shots whipped through the trees, and both beast and bullet tore a new path as they rocketed off into the distance.

Footsteps hurriedly approached. Two men knelt beside the Alex's crumpled body, checking him with concern for his well-being. They inspected his injuries while speaking quickly in their native tongue, which even in his strongest mental state would have been too foreign for him to understand. He felt them tie splints to his legs. By the feel of the awkward wideness and tinges of metal, he imagined it was their rifles that now held him together. His limp body offered no struggle as the hunters lifted him up, carrying him between them as they moved to waiting horses.

There was a cart, flat and level, that accepted his body and swallowed him whole. The men flipped up a door at the Alex's feet to keep him secure before the horses lurched ahead and departed the Red Forest. His body bounced in the back as they rode through the uneasy terrain, the venomous clicks of the Geiger counter screaming danger from its half-buried resting place.

As the wagon rolled up onto the pavement, speeding toward Pripyat, the mighty monolith of Chernobyl sat openly on its throne only a short distance away, ominously staring down at him as his world went dark once more.

*

Alex felt static in his ears as his head rolled around on the bed of the wagon. Quick, rapid jolts of energy jumped through him like electricity. His body leapt upward before flattening back onto the wagon with a hard thump. He heard the men shouting at him indistinctly. The cold night air strangled him while Chernobyl loomed, awaiting him and inviting his doom.

Shuddering, Alex recalled the beast again, and even felt the wind from its seeking nostrils still upon him. Despite the constant rolling rhythm of wagon wheels, and the creaking wood beneath his body, he could hear the beast galloping out there, cloaked in shadows, circling the terrain and awaiting its opportunity to feed. Its legs crushed into the ground like a machine punching through the earth, which stank of smoke and death and the dried copper stench of blood.

Alex saw her again—a memory floating past his pained, crimson-stressed eyes—dressed in white like an angel and darting onto the road like a doe, fearful and unaware. She was majestic, yet tragic. Beautiful, yet entrenched with deep sorrow. Somehow he heard the soft inhale of her gasp as she realized she was bathed in the motorcycle headlight.

His memory skipped, and the angel's breath was soon overwhelmed by the heavy groan of scraping metal on pavement and the drone of spinning motorcycle wheels. Alex could no longer hear the wagon, and the cushion beneath his body was certainly not the wooden bed he had been placed in moments before. Had more time passed than he thought? Had he lost consciousness again?

His surroundings fled from his searching eyes, and Alex was greeted with only clouded images. The hunters' voices boomed, then faded into the background—near and far like a rolling wave on the beach. His body was adjusted roughly, and he felt himself mummified. All his pain amplified to the point of peace. It overwhelmed him until he felt nothing else.

When the world became clear again, Alex was alone in an ocean conjured by his imagination. It was unnervingly tranquil. The clear water filled atop nothingness. There was no wind for the pathetic sail attached to the plank he sat upon, and he wore a constant frown like a punished child. This was finality—the conclusion of his existence. This empty place waited for him to tip the boat, fall into the darkness, and drown.

His frown flattened. Alex felt his mind accept the symbolism of his present world, and despite his fear, he began to tip. Surprisingly—at the very moment when he felt the first kiss of the water against his legs, swelling onto the plank to claim him—a voice curiously rang out through the ether. At first the sound was unpleasant, like a banshee's echoing wail. Soon, though, docile tones began to form into a siren's song, moving through the musical mediums from gramophone to the private concert hall of his attention. Alex sat up in his boat and the water receded from the plank. Greater intrigue formed on his face. He briefly shivered when he felt the wind twist across the surface of the water, catching the sail.

Alex blinked again, and the image of the woman dressed in white hovered there above him, distorted in his eyes. She sounded as sweet as she had looked in the dull headlights of his motorcycle. She sounded like . . .

"Katya?" he whispered between worlds as life struggled up through his chest to push out her name.

The angel smiled faintly, a knowing sadness forever lingering there in the tiniest crease near her lips. "Rest," she advised, and he followed her ensuing lullaby into a deep sleep.

Chapter Two

Alex's vision was still blurry as he pushed himself up to face the looming chaos surrounding him. He was lying in the middle of a street as firefighters rushed past him, scrambling frantically. Chernobyl was glowing like the sun ahead of them, beams of blinding light spilling out from a crevice that split through the center of the structure.

Blue flames jumped in columns from the exposed reactor and arched into the Red Forest, exploding with arcane power. The Ferris wheel in Pripyat spun like a rotor blade as the populace lay frozen in their beds, their souls screaming in torment though their bodies remained motionless and unaware. He could hear them.

"This isn't real," Alex said in an attempt to jolt his body free of what he knew to be a dream.

Helicopters tore through the sky above him, some hovering above the roof of the nuclear power plant. Alex clenched his eyes shut and shielded his ears as best he could to keep the dust and noise at bay. Trucks rolled past him, carrying more men in to battle against the vicious reactor. They begged for water and mercy, but their bravery in the face of such catastrophe was the very definition of noble.

"I had family there," a woman's voice cut through the terror. It was Katya. All the tumultuous noise of the siege faded into the background of Alex's mind as he recalled her chilling tale. She'd uttered those words months prior, weak and pale on a hospital bed. It was the memory he feared most. It was the day Katya died.

"Some never left." With a darkened sense of humor, Katya added, *"And some drank the milk."*

"It's so sad," Alex said while the same words resonated in the air as he'd spoken them in memory. He turned, looking for the source of her voice but finding only the chaos of the Chernobyl meltdown. Tears filled his eyes as he thrashed about, shouting silent pleas, hoping it would end this horrid memory. His real voice went silent. The memory was the only sound.

He knew what was coming next.

"My grandmother used to tell me I had an old soul, same as hers," Katya continued, a whimsical beauty in the soft whispers of her voice. *"I wonder if we'll go there together? After . . ."*

"You're not going anywhere, Katya. They're going to get you help, you'll see."

"I hope you'll come and visit." It was as though her words were on a predetermined path. The strength to argue had passed. Now all that remained was courage to face what was next.

Alex sobbed in both dream and memory. "Katya," he managed through the pain in his throat. "Please don't go."

"Ya lyublyu tebya vsey dushoy, Sasha," she muttered in her original tongue, her fingertips lifting to caress his face.

But Alex did not recall their touch, because fate had already stolen her strength. Sound returned to the world, the roar of men and flame drowning his ears. Alex trembled, alone with his nightmares. With clenched fists, he turned to Chernobyl and shouted profanities.

In a flash of bright white and blue fire, Chernobyl shouted back.

The explosion rocked the very fabric of existence, sending Alex toppling back along the road. Men cried in surprise as they were overtaken by the light. The vehicles faded to static until there was nothing left on the road.

Alex stood slowly, terrified at the groaning sounds emanating from the reactor. It was from there that they stepped, their monstrous hooves slamming into the concrete and crushing debris in the path of their menacing march. Each of the beasts, like grandiose hounds, locked onto him with gleaming eyes of blood-red fury. Dirt and decay coughed from their limbs as they stretched.

The lead beast grew larger as it approached, and the pack lingered back to give it primacy. Staring a hole through Alex's soul, it growled lowly before its horrible black maw split open.

"Katya!" it bellowed, an enormous grin on its lips. Its head tipped toward the sky. The ensuing roar tore the images from Alex's mind, shredding reality until it was gone.

Chapter Three

When his mind could bear no further distress, a spark fired from within, igniting consciousness. Alex sat up on the mattress with a quick yelp, panting as his eyes fought against the brightness of day. The world was a vague, murky cloud, indistinct like illusions of sunlight through thick panes of uneven glass.

Reaching his hand to his hairline, he ran his fingers along the dampened cloth that was tied around the circumference of his head. Tiny streaks of water had run through his dark hair and down his face. A metal bucket with another cloth sat at his bedside. Lost and confused, Alex wondered if he'd been brought to some makeshift hospital, or the home of a doctor.

Suddenly, the realization of the circumstances that brought him here forced him to briefly panic. Disturbing flashes of memory skipped through his thoughts, and he was immediately aware of his injuries. The sound of the motorcycle engine moaning its sad defeat played over and over again in his ears, causing him to tremble as he recalled the impact that followed.

Strangely, though, his body did not feel as damaged as he would have expected. In fact, he felt no pain at all. Someone had removed his jacket and boots, leaving him in his white T-shirt and faded blue jeans, though they had adopted some new tatters and rips along with some mud stains from his fall. His skin should have been littered with cuts and bruises, but he was in perfect form. Even the cloth on his head apparently served no purpose other than to keep him cool, as he could feel no injuries there, either.

Whoever had helped him was currently absent. Only the tranquil stillness of the rustic home greeted Alex's post-traumatic stress, and soon his curiosity overwhelmed the madness of his arrival. He remembered her, too—or, at least, the voice of the woman who stayed by his side.

Alex recalled her as a dream, but her healing, warm voice felt real enough in his mind. Whether it was soothing or haunting caused him some internal debate, as if some foggy remnant sat in the back of his mind attempting to remind him of the prophetic events that had forced him from his slumber.

He felt strange as he called her memory forward. The very idea of the woman's face churned fondness within him, as though he ought to know every detail of her life.

So why couldn't he remember her name?

It was curious, too, that when he sat on the brink of death, she was waiting there for him. She stayed with him. She held him in her arms and sang a heavenly tune to bring him the peace he so desperately needed. Anything to relieve the pain that threatened to steal him forever.

It felt like déjà vu, though he could not recall why.

Other things started to fade from the forefront of his mind as the minutes ticked away. He could hear the motorcycle engine, but he could not identify it. It reminded him of a bee soaring too close to his ear. He wondered if he'd ducked from some swarm of flies and clumsily bumped his head, because he could not for the life of him understand why there was a cloth at his hairline.

In the quiet, foreign strangeness of his new surroundings, Alex became aware of his solitude. The tranquility of the sunlit room was no longer welcoming, but rather unnerving. As he began to focus on the details, an odd familiarity overcame him. The bedroom was quaint and open to the rest of the small home. It felt more like a cottage—square and altogether smaller than average Western preference. The design was completely utilitarian, every item harmoniously set as a fundamental household necessity.

The floorboards creaked beneath his bare feet as he rose from the bed, beside which he discarded the cloth into the pail. Even in its seemingly old age, the cottage held a desirable, youthful charm. From the red hand-towels in the kitchen to the vase of roses on the dining table, the open room felt alive. In fact, most all the accents were red— unnaturally vibrant, exuberant, and passionate—and the dark brown wood of the floor and walls granted the homely warmth of a crackling fireplace. Alex regarded these details carefully as he assessed his caregiver, hoping she would live up to his expectations.

Collecting a pair of boots from the space beside the entryway that looked to be his size, Alex prepared himself for the outside world. Much like the floorboards, the front door opened with a chattering creak that resembled a woodpecker. He covered his eyes from the abundance of daylight that poured in. The angles the windows faced, or perhaps the dark wooden interior deflecting the sun's harshness, contrasted sharply to the brilliance of the outside world. Two insects, or small birds, whipped past Alex's face, and in his startled awe he flailed his arms above his head.

The sound of their passing reminded him of that droning noise he'd recalled earlier.

The streaks of white settled outside of range, hovering in the air and staring back at him. Once his eyes fully adjusted to the outside light, he focused on the creatures that looked at him with the same fear and confusion he offered. They were certainly not insects or birds; in fact, they were people, or at the very least shaped like people. Tiny and nude, with skin that appeared as porcelain, the floating creatures could have fit in the palm of his hand. If he were to catch them, their soft white glow would enrapture him like a child trapping a firefly.

Alex wasn't sure how to react to the sight of the fairy-like creatures, and instead of a proper question he babbled ignorantly. Despite their lack of wings, they flew in zigzags through the air with tiny trails of light that faded as dust in their wake. They continued to remain outside of his reach given his initial hostilities, but they seemed fascinated by him. When he extended his hand again, they darted off in separate directions, disappearing from view.

"Don't mind the berehyni," called a woman's voice from his left. There was an intimacy in her tone that calmed him.

Turning to greet her, Alex aimed his finger at the runaway creatures. "A what? A be . . . a bear—what?"

"Berehyni," she repeated. "Those fairy creatures you see. They are each a berehynia; berehyni means more than one." Clutching a broom in her hand, the woman had apparently been going about her daily chores. She appeared simple enough in her plain blue and yellow dress, which would be considered old-world compared to his fashion.

Still, he could not help but notice how the dress hugged the curves of her hips, or the small beads of sweat on her cheeks that reminded him of dew trickling down a lemon in a way that made him thirsty. The muscles in her arms and legs were faintly outlined as she worked, but the dress softened her visage. Her hair was as blonde as sun-kissed wheat and her blue eyes were as bright as crystal. She was stunning, youthfully energetic, and entirely too cozy a sight. "Lemonade," he whispered.

The woman's tone was calm though mixed with genuine concern, her accent faint but lyrical. "How are you feeling?" She looked him over to assess any residual damage. "Your head . . . you fell very hard."

Alex's thoughts raced as he started to question his sanity. Rubbing his hands against his eyes, he continued to feel jolted by the beauty of the unnaturally vivid tones of color that painted the world around him. But a fog hovered around the corner of his eyes, so heavy in its pull that he was convinced he was equal parts awake and locked in a dream. "Um, Miss . . . ?"

"Elena," she offered with a smile.

"Elena," he repeated, the name sounding foreign in his ears but easy on his tongue. With a deep breath, he collected himself while she patiently waited. "You watched over me."

Her eyes softened. "All night, yes."

"And you sang to me?"

"I . . . thought it would help," she said with some embarrassment. "I'm surprised you remember."

"It's about the only thing I remember," he admitted with

a sigh. The effects of his slumber, and his injuries, had not yet released him to normalcy. And certainly, this strange world did nothing to alleviate the burdensome questions in his mind. "I don't even know where to start."

"Start with what feels right."

"Well . . . where I am is the most obvious, but my parents would scold me from the grave if I didn't thank you first."

She waved her hands at him, shaking her head. "It's quite all right. I felt responsible, so . . ."

"Responsible? How?" he asked, unsure of her meaning. "Did you push me?"

Elena's eyes darted off as she winced. "No, I . . ." She cleared her throat and began pushing her broom around aimlessly until she could compose herself. "I'm responsible for the well-being of everyone here, of course."

Alex shifted about on his feet, his eyes glazing over as he looked out over the village surrounding them. He was not so unobservant that he couldn't tell he'd somehow,

26

inadvertently, struck a nerve. Regardless, he did not have the strength of will to pursue the topic just yet. "Can you tell me what happened? I don't . . . I can't remember anything."

"Not anything?" A frown weighed down the edges of her lips, her tone still shaken from his previous query. Elena stared into his eyes as he lost himself in the world, blanketing himself in its welcoming arms. She understood the look on his face. It was the same she had worn every day of her life. "You fell and hit your head in the forest. The woodsman found you and brought you to me, and now you are here."

Alex accepted each new piece of information as logical, though the lack of detail troubled him. He merely assumed she didn't know the full tale. "You speak really good English," he interjected.

Her lips twitched into a grin, though her furrowed brow indicated her confusion at the mere suggestion. "You're an odd fellow," she declared, shaking her head. "I assume your parents gave you a name?"

Embarrassed by his rudeness, he blushed. "It's Alex."

"Shall it be Alex then, or Sasha?" she asked coyly.

Elena's endearing smile continued to take him by surprise, and it was becoming an intoxicating thing to behold. Despite whatever obvious tension existed, hidden somewhere in his shaken memory, he had already grown quite fond of her. "Whichever you prefer," he replied, wondering if her suggestion for the diminutive meant she also felt somewhat distant.

Bouncing and posturing on her feet like a schoolgirl, Elena's pointer finger tapped on her lips as she pondered. "Well, as you are a guest in my home, I feel a formality is appropriate. But then again . . . Oh, Sasha just feels better."

Alex's eyes lit up. "I feel like someone used to call me that."

His exuberance brought some pain to her face, but she restrained herself. "You really hit your head, Sasha."

"I guess so," he said, feeling some pain once she called attention to it. There was a delay between his mind and his mouth. Fresh thoughts and memories were becoming difficult to recall. "There was a cart, I think. I was lying in the back, and it hurt because I kept bouncing."

She nodded. "The woodsman picked you up and brought you home on the back of his cart." With humor, she added, "You were meant to be a deer."

"I'm sorry," he said, though with equal frivolity in his voice. "The woodsman, he's a hunter? Were there rifles? I remember shots, I think."

Elena shifted around again, a discomfort brewing in her chest. "I imagine so. He wanted to talk to you when you woke up. Since he was in the forest, maybe he saw something? I wish I could tell you more, but . . ."

Alex took a deep breath and stared out at the village. The colors of nature were so amazingly exaggerated that they appeared to be conjured from watercolors, abstractly strung together to human familiarity. The sunlight was a constant flare of white through trees that were far too green.

"Maybe it's the concussion, but it's so beautiful here, today," he said slowly, smiling without concern. His choice of words visibly startled her, but he did not seem to notice. "I hope it's this beautiful every day."

"It will be," Elena said.

He smiled at her, even as she began to look distracted again. Clearing his throat, Alex assumed he had worn out his welcome, or perhaps it was the butterflies in his stomach at her very sight that made the situation uncomfortable. "So, this woodsman. Where can I find him?"

"Out in the woods, beyond the houses." She aimed her finger at the path for him to follow. "Be mindful of the traps. I'm sure he's not expecting you so soon."

"Tr . . . traps?" Alex asked.

"He *is* a hunter, Sasha." She giggled. The jovial nature of her response reassured him that perhaps he had given too much unnecessary thought to the burden of his presence. "When you come back, maybe we can talk more. You are still welcome here as my guest. Unless you have some other place to rest your head?"

Alex was overjoyed by her courtesy, or perhaps simply by the thought of seeing her again. Still, her voice shook the foundations of his memory. He could hear it in singsong, in melodies echoing in the distance. Perhaps it was merely that she had kept him alive. Brought him *here*.

As he trotted down the simple steps to the path leading from her house, he offered a wave back at her. "Maybe the woodsman will let me bring you something for dinner. It's the least I can do to repay your hospitality." In this demeanor, Alex felt like the schoolboy to her schoolgirl.

Elena clutched her broom again, looking off after him as he wound down the path and into the village. A berehynia fluttered in front of her face, hands on its hips as it glowered. Elena smacked her hand through the air to scare it into retreat. "It's none of your concern!" she barked. But as they both watched him leave their view, she sighed heavily, her shoulders dropping. "It's mine."

Chapter Four

Birds were chirping, and Alex heard their song during his entire journey, though he never saw any of them. It was like trying to catch water boiling while you're staring at it. They must have been hiding in the trees, but still emboldened enough to sing their tune. Everyone Alex saw along the way was toiling away on some daily chore, but they all stopped to give him a nod, a wave, or a smile. He felt so at home, so at peace that he had to remind himself that he didn't know any of them and that he hadn't lived here his entire life.

Their lives were simple and pastoral. Trenches were dug in from the nearby river to irrigate the farms and flower gardens. It seemed every house had at least one shovel leaning against the side. Alex admired their self-sufficiency. And the flowers! They seemed even more radiant in the open air than they'd been in Elena's home, though they still immediately drew his mind back there, and to her.

At the edge of the small town, the gouache world seemed to fade slightly. The town had held an almost literal glow of warmth and familiarity, and Alex felt its absence. On one side, tiny breeze-induced ripples rocked the surface of the glassy river, which glittered in the sunlight like crystals. On his other side, in the near distance, were buildings of some sort. They were solid, square, and gray. Simplistic. Concrete. There was a gloom that settled over the place like a cloud. He hesitated to look away from it for fear that it may reach out and take him should he be caught unaware.

The other town was a stark contrast to the place where he awoke. It was also familiar, but in a different way. Alex regarded it as a common industrial locale, with architectural efficiency that seemed planned with machine perfection in mind. There was a whistle in the breeze the longer he watched the shadows trail across the buildings, and he started to feel nervous, so much so that he sought comfort in the forest ahead.

As Alex proceeded into the forest, there was a thick canopy of trees above that cloaked the moist ground from the blinding gleam of sunlight. Alex stepped carefully, remembering Elena's warning, each step a heavy thud that shook his ears. Everything here was amplified to an extreme, likely due to his fearful anticipation that his foot would be chewed ferociously by some steel-toothed trap.

Despite the afternoon hour, Alex found his surroundings growing darker the further he traveled. It felt as though the world meant to surprise him with a sudden dusk. The forest swallowed the outside world, keeping it out of sight and reach with tangled branches and numerous tree trunks. A fog rose from the earth, coating it like a still blanket of snow. Alex froze, scanning the terrain with extra care.

"Hello?" he called helplessly, hoping for any sign of the woodsman. Daring not to take another step in blindness,

Alex lowered himself toward the ground. "Mr. Woodsman, sir, I don't know where you are! I lost the path!" As he spoke, he started to focus his mind on that very point. Was there ever a path? Where was he to look in this forest? Such obvious details had never crossed his mind until he was suffering the consequences of their absence.

Silence followed. The lovely song of the birds was gone. No water-colored majestic swirls painted this place. Alex sat in a cold, damp fog of muddied white, with only the decrepit browns and putrid greens of a mossy forest to welcome him.

A rustling sound came, bringing him hope. Alex chirped a greeting as bushes shifted, until the rest of nature followed suit and joined the dance. The forest seemed to literally tremble around him, and he could not deny that fear churned similar reactions in his muscles. Fight or flight instincts began to rise in him, and then something broke through the thicket.

It was fast, a blur of all the colors in their midst. But then he saw the tusks, aimed downward in a joust as the creature aimed to trample and impale him. Alex shouted, diving backward into the earth. His head found purchase on a fallen trunk of considerable thickness, which sent his vision into a frenzy.

He clamped his eyes shut to blind himself from the pain of keeping them focused. The last memory Alex could recall of that moment was the locomotive charge of the animal coming for him, then the booming call of lightning that shook the world around him.

*

A memory shook his consciousness. He remembered a beast stalking him, and the rifle shot that followed. Last time, he awoke in the quiet beauty of Elena's cabin home. When Alex's eyes twitched this time, an orange and yellow glow was shining into them. He weakly held up his hand to cover the source, then yanked it back as the flame teased its heat onto his skin. Groaning, he pushed himself upward, then released a shout at the sight of the man before him.

Grunting, the woodsman slammed the candle onto the table beside the hay-bed where Alex now sat. The grisly man was huge with broad shoulders and rigid arms, but a pouch sat happily on his belly that made him seem almost jolly. It would have, anyway, had he not worn an apron absolutely covered in blood.

"You hit your head much, boy," he bellowed from behind a scruffy salt-and-pepper beard, then turned back to his tools and his task. With heavy, hammering arms, a meat cleaver landed and split open the boar that he was preparing.

Alex saw the same tusks that came for him on the dead animal's face. The woodsman had arrived just in time, or perhaps he had been there the entire time, waiting for his meal. It must have been the call of his rifle that shouted thunder before the boar slammed into the ground beside Alex's fallen body in the forest.

Rubbing his head with embarrassment, Alex could only manage a chuckle. "Well, at least this time I did not cost you a meal."

"No," the woodsman agreed. "If you stay with us, you

have a promising career ahead of you as animal bait."

"Surely I have some other use?" he asked, his neck ducking with each hacking thump of blade through beast flesh.

The woodsman worked his craft with speed, the conversation giving him no pause or distraction. "Not yet." He spoke in short, simple phrases out of necessity. He was not a man who dabbled in fireside philosophy or idle chatter. "You hungry?"

Alex felt the grumble in his stomach. "Yes, please!"

"Good, you'll take the boar back to town for the feast."

This news deflated Alex's spirit. "Oh. Y-yes, sir. I will." He watched the hunter clean his weapons and prepare the animal for transport, ready to be placed over a spit. Once the woodsman had finished, he broke a loaf of bread in half, throwing the second piece to his guest. Alex fumbled with it, but managed to keep his hands on it, nibbling at inside scraps and trying not to think about the bloodied hands that offered it to him. "You wanted to meet with me, sir?"

"Stop calling me that."

"I'm sorry. Do you have a name?"

"Not one that anybody remembers."

Alex was daunted. "Then, what do I . . . ?"

"You will call me the woodsman, or you will just speak," he instructed matter-of-factly, with no room for confusion. "Now, what do you remember?"

As he told his tale, Alex thought the woodsman looked bored and disinterested.

"Before that?" the woodsman asked.

"Before I woke up?"

"Before anything." He watched the riddle plague Alex's mind. "You've always been here. This is your home, and it always will be. Do you know that?"

Despite the gaps in his mind, none of that sounded correct. "I don't remember that at all," Alex admitted, looking up to the woodsman with his lost, distant stare.

"That's why I'm telling you," he replied, unwavering in his convictions. "There was a fire in the Wormwood Forest. You went to fight it, and it beat you. And before the animals could claim you, I pulled you from their jaws." Even as Alex started shaking his head in disbelief, the woodsman insisted. "That's what happened."

"I don't . . . I don't know if that's true."

"Can you prove it isn't?"

"No, I suppose I—"

"Then it's true," the woodsman concluded, sloppily pouring himself a glass of vodka from an open bottle on the table where his bread sat. He drank it quickly, exhaling coolly. "And now, since you're a fireman, I am confident you can start a controlled blaze for the town supper so that we may roast this pig."

Alex watched the lines drawn out before him with more anger than curiosity. He felt himself a puppet—a toy to be tossed between the children of this town in order to amuse them long enough to give their parents reprieve. Still, the nature behind each statement was not false. He could not prove that any word of it was a lie, even if he felt he was being handed a script.

"I don't think I believe you," he finally said.

The woodsman chuckled in his deep, gruff, joyless voice. "Crises of conscious should be addressed to the damned priest. I just hunt meat."

Finally losing his patience, Alex smacked his hand on the table, discarding the candle with some satisfaction. "Why won't anyone tell me the truth?"

Marching toward him, the woodsman lifted his boot and crushed the fallen candle, snuffing its flame. "Because people are scared!"

"So am I!"

Grasping Alex by his shirt, the woodsman lifted him from the floor and shook him with great ferocity. Still, the complacency held solid in his voice as though he were sitting at the table with a pipe, calmly sipping his vodka. "Then stop spitting demons into your fantasies."

Alex coughed, pushing himself away with little success. It wasn't until the hunter released him that he gained any ground. "What the hell are you talking about?"

"Three days!" he barked, looking like one of his hunted

beasts as he stretched his arms out and roared. "For three days you laid in that damn bed spouting nonsense. Each day, my apprentice sat by your side and listened to your stupid dreams, your incoherent babble. And now he tells the priest the demon dogs are among us."

The very idea sent Alex's mind spinning. He recalled something similar, some ghastly voice booming a name in his ear, but the dream—the nightmare—continued to escape his recollection. He tried not to focus on it, but to no avail. "What animal was it that you found when you came upon me?"

To say that the woodsman matched Alex's anger would be an understatement. He far exceeded it. "You were a fireman in the Wormwood Forest. You fell. You hit your head. There was so much blood that you conjured fantasy and filled the heads of innocent morons with your foolishness."

"You didn't answer my question."

"I didn't see the damn thing!" The woodsman slammed

his fist against the wall, leaving a dent in the solid wood as he admitted his folly. "And if I had, I would not have missed any shot I sent against it. The woodsman does not miss!"

"So," Alex said, slumping back onto his hay-bed, "you don't know what really happened to me, either. Or what was out there."

After a short stare, the woodsman reached out and smacked Alex upside the head, which struck him with a satisfying yelp. "Dmitriy, my apprentice, is an ass—no, an ass would work harder in the fields. He is simply the wagon upon which you pile your superstitions, and I won't have any more of it. Now get up, fireman."

Pulling up to his feet, Alex rubbed the side of his head where he could still feel the sting of the woodsman's bear-sized hands. "Where are we going?"

The woodsman scowled at him, then grabbed for his rifle. "We are taking supper to our people, because God be damned if I will let you ruin another meal."

Chapter Five

Alex walked with the woodsman, who was still lecturing him on fires and pigs. Though the man was narrow in his conversational choices, there was a warmth to him that projected good nature. The impact of that mood was apparently contagious. Birds once again chirped invisibly in the thicket surrounding them, pleasantly singing their farewells to the day. The forest was far more vibrant and alive despite previous conditions, though it remained shady.

"This is a happy change," Alex said, his head swiveling

about as he took in the sights with greater optimism.

The woodsman grunted, halting his footsteps to set down the cart of boar meat he was hauling. "The lisovyk was not happy with you before."

"Lisovyk?" Alex repeated, his ignorance obvious, though his pronunciation had improved since his last attempt with Elena. He stopped to look at his companion for clarity.

"Spirit of this forest," the woodsman explained, politely resisting the urge to insult the boy's lack of culture, though his grumpy nature had encouraged him to do so. "He was not sure of you. He led you in circles and stole the light from your path until he made his decision. You're lucky I was there when he loosed the boar on you."

Alex's brow wrinkled as he played back the events in his mind. "Why would this lisovyk be angry with me?"

Sighing, the elder looked off in the direction of the dark walls of concrete Alex had seen on his way to the forest, though they were not yet visible through the trees. Their presence was known even when unseen. "He has not heard from his brother in the Wormwood Forest for some time now. I found you there too, and he must have wondered if you were somehow connected to the disappearance."

"But I was hurt there. If there's trouble in the forest, I think it found me along with . . . whatever else was there."

"And what happened before that?" The woodsman stared at the boy, but ultimately shook his head. "You don't know, and I don't know. I found you there without the blood of a forest spirit in your hands, so that will have to do, for now."

"Woodsman," Alex began, pausing briefly as he considered this new reality more openly for the first time, "what else did you find in the Wormwood Forest?"

The hunter was disarmed by the respect and humility in Alex's voice. The boy was acclimating. And though it was a question already asked, this time the woodsman did not react so aggressively. "There was something. You, as well, alongside of it. And you're still there."

"I am?"

"In your memories, fireman," he replied with a snap in

his tone. Something about the event was haunting his eyes. They darted back and forth as he considered his own recollection of the events. "I shot it. I don't miss, boy. And I *didn't* miss, no matter what Dmitriy says. Whatever it was, it took a bullet in the shoulder, but I never saw the blood. There was something . . ."

Alex stared at him purposefully. He caught himself holding his breath. "What was it?"

"Maggots and dirt. Just a clump of it all, in a small steaming pile right there on the forest floor. I told myself it was fog. That I missed. That everything was a coincidence, but it wasn't." He inhaled slowly. "I shot death, and it bled death." The woodsman pulled up the cart with the prepared boar seated upon it and handed it to Alex. "Give an older man reprieve. I don't wish to carry this anymore."

Pausing for a few moments, it took considerable effort for Alex to busy himself with taking over the cart, testing his strength and the weight of the contents. Once comfortable, he began marching again, though he had to force his legs to move. The grit in the woodsman's voice was as true as the sun's light. It terrified him more than anything he'd ever felt.

"The longer I'm here, the more I forget," Alex admitted, another fear spilling out. But then, hope twinkled in his gaze. "And the longer still, the more this feels like home."

"It is the way of things."

Alex chuckled. "That's it?"

"Yes, that's it," the woodsman agreed, though condescendingly. "You make something yours, it becomes yours. Belief is what drives us. Why shouldn't this be your home?"

Alex did not have an answer, and the more he pondered the question, the more sense it made. He felt complacent in this new world, or perhaps this old world he'd always been in. "Why are we having this feast?"

The woodsman smiled, perhaps his first genuinely positive reaction since their meeting. "The Festival of Lights is in two days. Tonight, the feast. Tomorrow will be busy with preparations. Grow your stomach fat, for you will work like a beast come morn."

With a heavy sigh of regret and self-doubt, Alex continued to trudge along with the cart. "I don't remember the festival."

"Then you are in luck, fireman. Everyone remembers something at the festival."

They reached the edge of the forest, where the bright world awaited on the short stretch of flat land leading to the village. The amber colors of dusk began to mix into the sky like tiny licks of faded flame reaching up to take hold of eternity, clamoring to remain just moments longer. Then the colors of plum and smoke mixed into the air, injecting it like ink. Nightfall would not long follow.

Passing the final tree, Alex turned his head in the direction of his companion. "What will I—"

But the woodsman was nowhere to be seen. Instead, Alex stood alone in the fading light of day as the forest shook behind him. Lumbering tremors, like heavy footsteps, receded in the distance, followed by the galloping sound of animals channeling into its wake. There were groans echoing through the air, like some kind of bellow or horn.

A nervous chill spiked through his body, but Alex smiled faintly, lifting up his hand. "I hope you find your brother," he whispered in parting, turning back to his path.

*

The whole town hurriedly came out of their houses when Alex returned with the boar. Several men hauled the animal from the cart and shifted it onto the spit, which was already prepared in the center of the town. They wore huge smiles as they worked, each patting him on the back as they passed, which granted Alex a momentary sense of pride in what was otherwise the woodsman's accomplishment.

Elena waited outside her door, arms folded across her chest as she grinned happily at her returning guest. She had taken one of the roses from its vase and cut the stem down so she could wear it in her hair. Her image was heavenly as Alex fixated on the details. While he politely greeted the other villagers as he passed, his path was direct to her.

"I brought dinner," he said.

She nodded. "I can see that. And the woodsman?"

"I don't think he'll be joining us."

The news did not faze her. "He never does. Did he help you remember anything?"

Alex's lips pursed as he glanced about uncomfortably. "He said I'm a fireman."

Elena giggled, then covered her lips quickly before clearing her throat. "I'm sorry, that was rude."

"What? I don't look the part?" he asked with some amusement, gesturing to himself.

She bobbed her head from side to side, scrupulously inspecting him as she played along. "You are quite fit, but I cannot imagine you with an axe and a pail of water." They each laughed, shifting about in front of one another like young lovers embarrassed of their own pretenses. "You know, fireman, you are expected to light the fire for our feast."

His eyes popped wide. "I thought he was kidding."

"Not a fan of ceremony?"

He patted himself over. "Well, it's not that I can't. It's just that I'm fresh out of matches."

Elena laughed heartily. Her cheeks were pink and her eyes lazy, and crimson streaks painted her lips. She had been drinking, but Alex only noticed when she moved closer to take him by the hand, leading him back toward the spit. "Come, I will show you."

Alex followed along with his own blush. "You realize how embarrassed I am to have a lady light a fire for me?"

Elena stopped and turned to face him. She was standing closer than he expected, and he nervously bit the inside of his lip. "What do you know about the zhar-ptysia?" she asked.

Alex could not even manage to repeat the name, despite several attempts. "N-nothing," he finally admitted.

"Then how can you be expected to light a fire?"

The inquiry would disparage him for some time before he made peace with his confusion. Elena positioned him beside the spit with the dead boar prepared neatly atop freshly chopped logs. Everyone in town began to gather, putting their chores, their tools, and any other unfinished business aside for another day. Their faces regarded him as family, and though he didn't recognize any of them, he felt as though he should. This *was* his family, because they believed it, as the woodsman had said.

Alex was starting to believe it, too.

"Now, stand here," Elena instructed. "Hold up your hands to the sky."

Obeying her instructions, Alex felt silly in his newfound posture. The gesture was so pained that he heard several snickers from his new family. "Okay. Now I pray it doesn't rain?" he asked mockingly.

"If you wish," she replied, placing a bag in his hand. "Open this."

Clutching the small burlap, Alex tugged at the string holding it together at the top seam. When the tiny sack opened, a glow of fire entered the air. He actually managed to duck a bit, which of course churned more laughter from the crowd. "Now what?" he asked, becoming annoyed with himself.

"Put it on the logs!" Elena chirped brightly, also amused by his reactions.

Sighing, Alex reached into the bag and produced a single feather. It was brilliantly yellow and glowed a soft orange hue. Quite literally, it was a tangible flame. He stared, mesmerized. "What is this?"

"The logs, Sasha."

"Right." He set the feather down onto the wood. "And now I—"

Elena's arms grasped at his shoulders, interrupting him and pulling him several steps backward. Nearly stumbling, he looked to her with some concern before he heard the squawk in the sky.

It came as a streak of fire through the plum clouds, illuminating the sky in a small pocket surrounding it before the entire object streaked downward. There was a heavy channel of wind that slammed into the ground before them, causing a few excited gasps from the villagers. Then, when the air settled, Alex stared at the creature now seated atop the spit.

The bird cocked its head curiously, its elaborate and beautiful fan of feathers sashaying meticulously behind it. Everyone sat, quietly staring at the illumed peacock as though it were about to deliver a speech. Suddenly, though perhaps expectedly to everyone aside from Alex, the bird's head tipped downward to snatch the feather from the wood pile. Then, with a flap of its wings, fire brewed in the wind of its wake like a rocket, and it soared off into the sky with a whirlwind of heat.

A fire crackled softly beneath the now perfectly cooked boar, which sat awaiting the villagers' knives and forks. Though the bird had fled, there was still a tiny glimmer in the sky, like a dot of light circling aimlessly.

"Thank you, zhar-ptysia!" chanted one villager, and several others offered their praise as they began the feast.

Nudging his arm, Elena fondly pointed at the falling light in the sky. "It's another feather, fireman. You have to collect it and keep it until the next feast, so zhar-ptysia can join us again for supper."

"*This* is what it means to be the fireman!" he cried in disbelief, and with giddy amazement he continued to search the skies for the bird of fire, though it had completely disappeared. "A zhar-ptysia . . . I saw it! I don't even know what happened, but I can't tell you how amazing that was!"

Elena tenderly watched him, her cheek sloping toward her shoulder. She wore a smile so large that it pained her. A slickness formed around her eyes, but she clenched them shut and gave him a friendly shove. "Go get the feather, Sasha, or you will certainly need your matches in the future!"

Skipping forward, Alex was so filled with wonder that he didn't hesitate to follow her instructions. He jogged between a pair of houses, watching the feather roll down a roof and sail faintly down atop a grain pile. Hurriedly, he snatched it up before a gust of wind stole it from him. With childlike awe, he stared at the feather and its candlelight glow before pocketing it into the tiny sack that Elena had given him earlier.

When he turned back to his path, Alex gasped at the

sight of a man looming there, watching him with a stoic stare on his face. The man was older, his cheeks and eyelids chiseled with wrinkles that had formed from a permanently cast scowl. Around his neck was a thick golden chain that halted above his stomach, where a large wooden cross hung in plain sight.

"Are you malice?" the priest asked, his brawny body frozen sternly. "Are you temptation? Do you mean to mislead us?"

Alex's lip trembled. He struggled with his response. The night air strangled him as he stood equally motionless, feeling as though he'd been hunted and trapped. "M-my name is Alex, sir."

"What did he tell you, Alex?"

"Who?"

The priest sneered, the very sound of the man's name coated with bitterness. "*The woodsman.* What did he tell you about who you are, or who you were?"

Alex swallowed, clearing his throat. "He told me I'm the f-fireman."

"But you know that is a lie," the older man said in a tone so mocking, so scolding, he may as well have smacked Alex across the cheek. "You don't belong here. You come in the wake of demons and wreck all that ever has been."

Looking away, Alex clenched his fist and the sack within his palm until he realized the fragility of what he carried. He did not offer the priest another look, but shuffled past him to return to the feast.

"Go back to where you belong!" the priest called after him. "And may God have mercy on you for all that you have wrought and may yet still reap from us!"

Alex felt his feet shift faster, the old man's words punching his soul like a blacksmith's hammer. "I don't belong here?" he whispered, his mind caving as any memory of days gone escaped him completely. "Then where . . . ?"

When he made it back to the pig feast, Elena was standing with a group of villagers, laughing and sharing stories. A berehynia sat upon her shoulder, bobbing its head as it listened to the gossip. The tiny creature saw Alex and fluttered up into the air, soaring toward him.

The berehynia hovered just in front of his nose, staring at him. Though cloaked in foggy white light, Alex could see the somber frown on its face. Its shoulders sloped frailly as it glanced up into his eyes and then back to the ground. Such sadness veiled its otherwise exuberant existence, though it was a perfect reflection of Alex's mood following the priest's short talk.

Elena departed the group and walked over to him, throwing her arms around his neck and sinking low as she exhaled warmly. "Oh, Sasha. Is it time to go home yet?"

The gesture stole his breath and made his soul melt into a fondness so sincere that he felt as though he might faint. Alex lifted her gently, holding onto her waist to keep her standing. "Elena . . . where is this, really? Nothing makes sense to me anymore."

Lifting her gaze to him, her brow wrinkled in confusion before her face turned to anger. "Oh God, he spoke to you, didn't he? What did that ass say to you?"

"What? Who?"

"The priest!" she yelled. Several heads turned. "What was it this time? That you don't belong here?" Elena waved one hand angrily about in the air, shouting to the invisible recipient of her rage. "You must let the man move in before you can chastise him for missing your sermons!"

Alex shook his head. He was as amused as he was flustered. "Elena, no, it's not his fault. He just rattled me. I really can't remember anything. What if he's right?"

Cupping her angry fist into a flat palm on his cheek, Elena squeezed his face. "Look at me, Sasha. It's his way, do you understand? He is testing your faith and your resolve. If we all listened to his dog-bark, none of us would be here."

"But, honestly, do I belong here? Do you remember me? Have I always been here, Elena?"

She stared into his eyes for a long time. The background chattering seemed to fade away as her blue eyes shifted across his face, tears welling in them again. This time, she did not bother to suppress them. "I've known you forever, Sasha. And I've missed you so much."

When their lips drifted toward one another it was on instinct, as if their bodies moved by muscle memory. They kissed like reunited lovers, drowning in the scent and taste of each other. It was everything he knew, everything he'd dreamed of every night for as long as he could remember.

And this, he *did* remember.

Splitting her lips from his, Elena's eyes opened slowly, resting on his as she swayed her hips. The rose had fallen from her hair, unnoticed. "Take me home, Sasha."

There was a lingering scent of alcohol on her breath that made Alex pause. "Are you sure?"

"I am drunk on wine and loneliness, Sasha," she admitted. "And I don't wish to be alone tonight." Elena scoffed at him. "There, now you've made me speak bluntly. Are you going to deny—"

His lips were on hers again, only briefly, before he reassured her with a shake of his head. "I'm not. I won't." The pair departed the feast with their arms securely wrapped around one another, until they disappeared behind the door of Elena's home.

Left behind, the tiny berehynia watched with the same heaviness weighing its lips down sadly. It dropped slowly to the ground, where the rose that earlier sat in Elena's hair had fallen. Wrappings its arms around the petals, the berehynia and rose lost their telltale glimmer as they faded away into a dream together.

"I warned you," the berehynia hissed in a hushed tone from its tiny mouth.

Nothing could stop it from happening now.

They were coming.

Chapter Six

Pots. Clamoring, banging pots beat together like the angry percussion of war throughout the house as something akin to a bear howled. Alex woke and covered his ears at the abrupt, painful noise. Elena groaned, leaping from the bed with a sheet wrapped around her body as she stormed into the living room, shouting obscenities.

Sitting in bed, Alex rubbed at his temples to ease the dull the throbbing in his head as the beating began to fade. "What is happening, now?" he asked with a sigh.

"Here! Eat this!" Elena called from the next room. Alex heard the oven door open and something land within before the same door was slammed shut. She charged back into the bed, still muttering obscenities as she landed face-first onto the mattress.

Alex's eyes were bloodshot. "What, and why, and do I even want to know?"

"Damned domovyk is mad at me," she muttered, her face buried into the pillow. A single pot-clang rang out in retort from the other room. "Oh my God, my head . . ."

"Tell me about it," he agreed.

"You were not the one drinking!"

"Oh, right." He smirked sheepishly, squinting at the morning light creeping in through the window. "Please tell me we can go back to bed."

Elena growled, then pouted into her pillow. "We have to get ready for the festival."

Stroking her back, Alex nodded. "Yeah, the woodsman mentioned the festival. I still don't know what it is."

She rolled her head to rest her cheek on the pillow, looking up at him. "Every year, on 26 April, we celebrate a majestic and powerful flash of light. It's tradition. They say the villagers settled here because of the light they saw early morning on that day."

"Am I to light more fires?" he asked, some hope in his voice.

"Just help me move my flowers there. I have dozens of rose bushes to transport."

"Transport? Where?"

"Into Pripyat, of course," she replied, pushing up from the bed and moving into the bathroom to tidy her hair in the mirror. "We always go to Pripyat for the festival. That's where everyone was when the flash came, and that's why this village was founded here."

Alex shifted around uncomfortably. "That concrete town, that's Pripyat?"

Catching his uncertain tone, Elena poked her head out from behind the door of the bathroom. "Is something wrong?"

He blinked, glancing over to her. "It's just that . . . all of this seems familiar, somehow."

Stepping out from the bathroom, Elena had dressed herself in a simple off-white shirt and thick pants carrying snags from rose thorns. She was ready for her garden. Her hands were busy tying her blonde hair into a bun at the top of her head. "Everyone remembers something at the festival, Sasha. You will too."

Watching her move around the room, Alex frowned. She seemed different. The woman in his arms the night prior had drunk herself into a dream to escape some overwhelming sadness. But now, here she was, going about her business carefully choreographed in this play.

What was it that had weighed on her so heavily, now so easily forgotten? The other side of the coin frightened him, though. Perhaps she had not slipped into this demeanor, this lucidity, because of her actions last night. Perhaps she drank to *escape* this dream.

Alex felt the weight of that sink into his heart. Initially,

Elena had been distant, like she was peeling away from the painting of her life. There was paleness in her cheeks where everyone else had color. But the spell was coming back, as though she had forgotten the strange circumstances of their meeting. She was enraptured and claimed again. And worst of all, was he to blame for her change? Had the night they spent together trapped her soul back into this doll of her awakened self?

And then the thought dawned on him—a horrible nightmare that had not occurred to him before, but was now seeping into his senses and dripping like wax on everything surrounding him. Was he awake anymore, either?

Rising from the bed, Alex began to get dressed. The answer to that question faded into the background of his mind like so much else had since he awoke the day before.

"Do you have any gloves for me, Elena? I don't want my hands to sting when I hold you later."

"Stop it," she said with a silly smile on her face, leading him into the kitchen for breakfast.

They shared breakfast of bread with fruit and butter

along with tea and honey, and happily spoke like an old married couple in their daily routine. Alex tried to help her clean up, but she insisted otherwise. Each of them smiled almost constantly as they talked through the festival preparations.

Once outside, the garden was a beautiful, radiant crimson from the multitude of red rose bushes packed in baskets and ready for transport. Alex gathered the carts and they loaded them together.

"It's going to look beautiful," he said. "That dark place could use some color, anyway."

"Just wait until we get it all set up, Sasha. Pripyat will be a city of roses when we're finished."

Villagers came by to check in and wish them well. Some brought food for lunch and snacks for every other craving throughout the day. Others provided crates overflowing with decorations. There were pitchers of water, loaves of bread, and stacks of towels that made Alex feel as though they were preparing for a giant picnic, which was not far from the truth of it. The entire village had an excited energy as people started to move toward the nearby town.

With all the roses loaded, Alex and Elena each took a cart in their hands and started to pull. As they departed for Pripyat, Alex looked back to the house and saw the lingering shadow of someone, or something, standing there. It was large, coated in fur like an animal, and lifted a lumbering arm up into the air as it waved good-bye.

Alex turned around entirely, checking his vision, but there was nothing to be seen. Elena noticed his swivel.

"What was it?" she asked.

"Nothing, I guess." He shrugged. "Must have been my imagination." An uneasy feeling settled along his spine, but he shook it off and focused on the task at hand.

Narrowing her eyes at the nagging sensation, Elena glanced back to the house again, whispering to herself, "Damn domovyk."

*

Though seemingly dark from a distance, Pripyat was surprisingly clean—clinically so. The sunlight cast a simple glow on their monotone surroundings. If the world behind was a painting, this place was a charcoal sketch. Alex peered into windows as they passed, but from a combination of dust and daylight they were opaque.

It may as well have been a model for all the disturbing lack of life. Certainly, there were trees. Nature was groomed and kept in managed perfection. This place was a photograph masked and edited into a different thing.

It was a lie.

Elena touched her hand to his shoulder when she noticed his mood. He forced a smile for her in return, but this only brought her sadness to the surface. For some reason, seeing this side of her put him at some ease, as if she were returning to the person he met yesterday—as if she saw the lie, too.

Still, the villagers went along with their roles in the play. Everyone arrived at the center of the city, where an amusement park sat lonely and untouched. A soft wind blew through the illusionary world, barely carrying a sound as it sailed effortlessly through the polished steel frame of the Ferris wheel, the merry-go-round, and past them all into the trees and buildings around them.

Alex set down his cart in the same area as everyone else, where they began unloading their tributes. Despite the ominous worry that made him sluggish, he worked diligently with Elena to place the rose bushes in their potted baskets along the square. Outside the attractions was a line of trees in soil that made for easy planting. Several villagers helped dig. They smacked their shovels into the dirt beneath the twiggy trees with their plain green leaves. They said the shade would be fine for the roses.

Elsewhere around the square were manmade concrete walls that had been hollowed and filled with dirt. More bushes were planted there. They said the direct sunlight would be fine for the roses, too. Alex recognized their words as nonsense, scripted into their brains for use during festival preparation. The truth was simple: there would be roses, and they would be planted. The rest was inconsequential.

Children laughed and skipped around, playing on the amusement park rides as their parents worked. Blankets were laid on the ground for the upcoming picnic. The villagers produced paintings, pictures of family members, jewelry and similar tributes, and placed them onto the blankets, the merry-go-round seats, and the Ferris wheel buckets alongside flower wreaths. It reminded Alex of a shrine, or a grave, and made him uncomfortable.

One of the villagers complained of clouds, but the sky was as dull as the rest of the town. Alex stared up at it with squinted eyes. He could see nothing except a dim glow that reminded him of florescent light strips. Though after this revelation, he could not recall ever seeing such a thing in his life.

"This place is strange," he finally said.

Patting the dirt atop a planted bush, Elena looked at him. "The flowers will help. They will add some color."

"Do you feel it, too?"

She shook her head, but did not respond truthfully. "I don't know what you mean."

"It's just . . . everything here is so plain. So boring."

"Don't be insulting, Sasha."

He huffed, apparently failing to communicate his true feelings. "But where is everyone?"

"We're all right here," she replied, motioning to all the villagers hard at work.

"Yeah, but where is everyone that lives here? What's inside all the buildings?"

Elena frowned again, sitting back on her feet in her kneeling position as she stared at him. "No one here sees the difference. This is just what we do, where we go, for the festival."

His eyes forecasted apologies, though he averted actually speaking any aloud. "Were you like this before? Was everything like this before I came?"

"It's always been like this," she admitted with a low tone of regret. "But everything's been different since you got here. For me, anyway."

He chuckled in hopes to break some of the tension. "It's only been a few days. And I slept for most of them."

She was committed to the discussion. "Have you ever felt like you woke up in someone else's life?"

Alex's lips twitched as he looked away. "I've been swimming in amnesia since I woke up. Everyone is telling me who I am, or what to be, and I don't know if any of it is true. I feel like—"

"Like you're just watching it all play out in front of you?" she concluded for him.

"Yeah."

With a deep sigh, Elena pushed herself to her feet. "Nothing has been the same since I came back from the Wormwood Forest."

His eyes widened. "Wait, you were there? At the Wormwood Forest? When?"

Elena panicked at the question. "No, I'm sorry, I shouldn't have said anything."

"If you know something about my injury, Elena, you

have to tell me!"

Tears began to roll down her face. She sniffled, looking to him with a pained smile. "Sasha, I don't know if you are a fireman. I don't know if you've been with me for years or minutes. But I just want you to *be*. Here, with me, for as long as we can."

Torn with emotion, he didn't know if he should embrace her or run from her. It was clear that she knew more than she would admit. Their connection was undeniable, but he began to wonder about the depth of it. When did it start? How long had they felt this way? Was he a teenager in puppy-love, or a man with long-harbored feelings for this woman? He wished for a moment—a mere glimpse at clarity for the sake of sanity and his heart.

"Elena . . ." he began, but hesitated.

She looked to him expectantly, her face filled with hope that he would reciprocate the words, even if she already knew he held the feelings. But the words never came. Rather, they were interrupted by something more demanding of their attention.

There was a groan in the distance, vibrated from within iron walls, which rocked the very earth. Alex caught himself on the wall where the roses sat, Elena grasping onto him. The sky darkened, veins of red bleeding through the dull luminance of the florescent sun. Only the soft, pulsating glow of the roses around them kept the area brighter than the hue of the blood sky.

Tremors violently ripped across the ground again, until they disappeared as quickly as they began. The villagers complained, some of them fallen over in the disturbance. Surprise crept onto every face. This was not part of the preparations. This was something else entirely.

Finally able to get his footing, Alex stood and helped Elena to her feet. "Was that an earthquake?"

"Nothing like that has ever happened before," she said, her words punctuated with fear. "We have to check on everyone. There are children here!"

They separated and ran to the aid of their fellow villagers. After a few minutes, they heard an encroaching sound, like galloping horses but heavier. Alex knew that sound. It spoke to him as though it controlled him—owned him. His face paled.

"We have to run." It was barely audible. Pebbles shifted on the ground as the earth-pounding sprint grew nearer. Mustering the totality of his will, Alex roared so hard that his throat felt as though it had ripped on the inside. "*Run!*"

It was too late. The first beast charged onto the square. Though it thrived in the obscurity of shadow, there was enough light so that none would be spared the horror of the monster's appearance.

Alex remembered every detail of it, from its hulking shoulders to its dirt-caked body leaking smoke like a crushed campfire. The beast's red eyes left a streak of light as they darted about on its swiveling head. And then, it roared.

Clamping his hands to his ears, Alex began to spout pleas as the world seemed to disintegrate around him. The sky smoldered as rust, moss, and decay choked every rock, every building, and every amusement park feature around him. He ducked his head at the sound of a rotary engine screaming above. A helicopter loomed there. When it lifted higher, he heard a different form of screaming.

The villagers were dashing in all directions. Turmoil claimed everyone and everything. Flashes of gold streaked past Alex in the form of people sprinting, like beings of light dressed in static. These people, who had seemingly stepped out of memory, out of history, discarded their possessions in a hurry as they fled. The villagers now carried this strange vibrancy, too.

Everything phased in and out of this disaster. The scene went white again before it curdled brown with age and death, back and forth like a heartbeat. Flashes of memory streaked from every direction, fleeing in terror. Reality itself was coming apart at the seams. Alex finally took his own advice and sprinted away toward the buildings. He leapt through a thicket of rose bushes, the thorns ripping at his clothing and flesh as petals flew all over.

Behind him, he could hear the beasts and their clapping hooves against the pavement. A wayward glance saw more of the beasts on the other side of the wall of roses planted at the tree line. They were chopping their jaws, mud dripping from them as they lingered angrily. The villagers screamed, or perhaps it was this strange memory that seeped into Alex's consciousness. He was no longer certain which was real and which was clawing at his senses through the dream.

The dream. He remembered it now. The creatures coming from the reactor, and the groan that trumpeted their arrival. It was the same, only this time Alex was awake. Stumbling, he smacked through a cloud of memory, of people, and landed into someone quite real.

"Run, you fool!" the man shouted, pushing Alex aside and aiming his rifle.

Alex continued his sprint. Bullets shot out in repetition, then ended with a quick, shrill shout. One of the beasts was behind him, still charging. It must have barreled through the hunter to keep the chase.

Ahead of him, the building wall was mostly windows, and they phased back and forth between opaque plainness and open degradation. With no other choice, Alex blocked his face with his arms and leapt through.

But there was no impact. The dream must have phased again and let him sail through an open space. He landed in a stumble inside a gymnasium of some sort. The world was white again. A large pool sat before him, full of motionless water.

An explosion of glass met the monster's entry. Regardless of the state of the world, or the dream, it was here. Rattled, Alex darted forward and sprung for the pool water. Luck was not on his side this time, as the world shifted again and he fell straight to the mossy, concrete floor of the empty cavity.

Alex rolled in pain. He expected the world to blink again with another heartbeat change of reality. He wondered if he would suddenly find himself drowning at the bottom of the pool, but it never came. The pain kept him grounded. His body felt as though it were in shambles.

Above him, on the edge of the empty pool, stood the smoke-bleeding creature. It jumped down easily, the ground cracking beneath its impact. Then it marched toward him, its jaws snapping.

Pushing his back to the curve in the pool, Alex sat upright and faced the beast, which came so close to him that he could smell the rot from whatever lay beneath the disgusting exterior coat of this foul creature. But despite its low growl, its readiness, it did not leap at him. Instead, it stared at him as though kept at bay by some unknown force.

Raising a trembling hand into the air, cut by thorns and still holding rose petals on his sleeve, Alex begged the creature for mercy. It did not speak, but kept snapping at him like a dog angrily obeying a command to yield.

Alex yelped at the sound of a gunshot. Stumbling aside, the monster turned to the top of the pool and roared. It was the villager that had pushed him away just minutes ago. He was still alive, rifle at the ready and aimed down into the pool.

"Get away from him!" he barked bravely.

Alex reached into his pocket and freed the burlap sack still sitting within. The beast was distracted, pacing about the pool basin as it stared up at the hunter who continued to fire down. Each bullet separated pockets of mud and maggots from the monster, which landed in steaming piles, exactly as the woodsman had described.

Freeing the small tie around the sack, Alex produced the golden, glowing feather from inside. "Help me, zhar-ptysia!" he shouted at the top of his lungs, throwing the feather into the muck that coated the creature's body. It turned to Alex with wild eyes, roaring death into his face.

A new sound shrieked in the sky, a cry he recognized from the night before. Like a lightning bolt of fire, the zhar-ptysia landed on the back of the beast, head snapping down to pluck its feather free. Bucking wildly, the monster tried to free the bird from its back. Its teeth chomped to catch the bird's tail, but before it could find purchase, the feather ignited.

As if accelerated by gasoline, the flames rushed upward and outward. Alex cried out, reaching his hand for the villager who immediately disappeared behind a blinding curtain of orange and yellow. The pool exploded, leaving only a pocket around Alex. He huddled in a tight ball to avoid suffering the burning fate of the creature—and terribly, the villager—before him. The monster roared out so violently that Alex thought his ears might burst, but the wretched sound curdled into a bubbling nothingness as it turned to ash and collapsed in a pile of death.

Outside the gymnasium, the priest looked on as the fires spilled into the night. They swallowed a villager standing too near, instantly incinerating him. Aghast and disgusted, the priest waited, staring into the open building. Eventually, the zhar-ptysia soared off, back into the sky and out of sight, followed by a hobbling Alex, who clutched another glimmering feather in his hand as he fell and wept to the pile of ash where the villager once stood.

"Demon!" the priest hissed in a whisper, clutching his cross and rushing back toward the village.

Alex slowly lifted his head and looked around. The bleeding sky began to fade, and light crept back over Pripyat. Departing after the death of their pack comrade, the beasts disappeared to regroup, but Alex was certain they would return.

Pushing slowly to his feet, a breath caught in his chest. His limp turned to a hurried hop as he fought through the pain to return to the makeshift square. He could see villagers still fleeing in the distance, but piles of steaming clothes were littered about the amusement park. He started grabbing at them, checking them for familiarity. Alex could not fathom what befell their former owners.

A smog of death hovered above the ground, keeping his vision limited. The zhar-ptysia's feather was a weak torch. He scrambled. His heart stopped. And then, there she was.

Elena sat on her knees in the center of the square. In her hands were two rose stems, which she gripped so tightly that blood seeped between her fingers. She looked up at Alex and began to cry, dropping the flowers and reaching out to him.

Alex collapsed to the ground and wrapped his arms around her, and together they rocked in the wake of the slaughter.

"Why?" she bellowed.

He cupped her head into his folded arm, burying her cheek into his chest as he tried to calm her. "I don't know, Elena."

"No!" she objected, pushing him back. There was anger in her reddened eyes. "Why didn't they take *me?*"

Chapter Seven

Elena sat on a blanket by the riverbank. Darkness had already claimed the night sky, leaving only faint starlight twinkling down through the sea of black. Though she felt no immediate danger, she was nervous, and when Alex's foot crunched down on a branch in the close distance, she gasped.

"It's only me," he whispered, pausing his approach until she relaxed. "You shouldn't be out here anyway, if you're that afraid of them coming back."

"They won't," she said in a voice that offered no reassurance. "Their bellies are fat with our losses, and they needn't ride out for food when they can just claim us tomorrow during the festival."

Alex sat down on the blanket beside her with a grunt, nodding as he looked out onto the placid, glassy water. He set down a pair of rose stems beside her. "You're more right than you know." He had come from a town meeting Elena had insisted he attend without her, as she could not bear to see anyone.

"What did they decide?" she asked.

He smirked. "I don't even know why they framed it like a discussion. Everyone's just screaming for bloodshed. The woodsman is going to lead them all with rifles to defend the festival."

"That surprises me."

"He said if everyone was so eager to die, he'd be happy to play shepherd. Less mouths to feed in the future."

She sneered, staring at the blanket beneath them. "Never mind. That does sound like him."

"Elena . . . what happened back there, today?"

"Did you tell them about the roses?" She raised her gaze to him, motioning to the stems he brought with him.

Alex watched her carefully, assessing the meaning behind her question. "I told them I saw the monsters pacing outside the row of roses we planted, as if they couldn't get through. And that when I was face-to-face with one of them, but covered in petals, it did not bite me."

Elena nodded, returning to her downward stare. "Thank you."

"They think they have a fighting chance now. Everyone is pinning roses to their chests. I saw some women sprinkling petals on their doorstep when I snuck out to find you." He offered her a humored glance. "I think your garden is ruined, Elena."

"I don't think I'll need it anymore," she admitted vaguely before curling up into a ball. Her head used his leg as a pillow. "I owe you an explanation."

Alex relaxed his leg muscles in order to serve as a more

comfortable resting place. "Only if you're ready."

After a moment of hesitation, Elena nodded. "I was in the Wormwood Forest that night." She rolled her head and looked up at him. "I was looking for you."

Alex felt his heart skip. He looked around quickly, trying to piece together the situation. "But then . . . does that mean . . . Have I always been here, in this village?"

"No, that's not what happened," she replied sadly, sniffling as she took in a deep breath. "I used to have these dreams. My whole life, I've always been torn between this place and another. I never remember much about them. Where I am or what I see—they're just dreams. But you . . . your face . . . I kept seeing it. I knew I'd find you that night if I went looking for you. I knew you'd be there."

"And you did," he uttered quietly. "So you were the one who found me."

"But I was scared. When I saw you, I was so terrified that I ran through the forest, as hard as I could. I went all the way to the woodsman and told him that I heard something on my walk."

He ran his fingers idly through her hair, forcing himself to do so in order to remain calm and focused. "Why were you scared of me?"

"Have you ever had a prophetic dream come true, Sasha? It was terrifying to think I might be losing my mind as I ran off into the night. But then to find you . . . I knew I would suffocate from exhaustion before my legs stopped. I still can't believe it happened."

All he could do was nod. "So then the woodsman found me . . ."

"And brought you to me to take care of you. He never said anything about it after that. Just that you should come see him when you woke. I think he left you with me to teach me some lesson. Make me take responsibility for my actions. I don't know." Elena paused, reaching her arm up to tuck her hand behind his head. "You weren't alone when he came for you though, were you?"

"No," Alex confessed. "I wasn't."

"Was it one of those creatures?"

"At the assembly, the priest called them the 'shadow hounds'. As if people weren't afraid enough without a moniker like that." Alex shifted on the blanket, putting his weight on his opposite leg. "He was staring at me the whole night. Guy gives me the creeps."

Elena sighed, feeling another rush of emotion flood through her body, clenching its angry fist around her heart. "Can they really not be stopped? Is this . . . is this the end, Sasha?"

There was a pause as he briefly considered not telling her. Truth be told, Alex wished he could have forgotten the details completely. "They can be killed."

She sat up quickly, spinning and looking at him. "What? How?"

Reaching his hands up to calm her, he looked away uneasily. "I called zhar-ptysia to save me. It turned the shadow hound to ash."

"Alex!" she shouted, smacking at his chest. "We have to tell someone!"

"No! Damn it, Elena! Listen! It also . . . One of the

villagers was there, too. He was caught in the fire. Zhar-ptysia saved me, but . . . someone died."

Elena's mouth fell open as she slumped back into helplessness. She buried her face in her hands and started to cry again, though in truth there were no tears left to shed. Alex hesitated, his hand hovering awkwardly in the air, torn between a desire to comfort her or succumb to his own bubbling sadness.

When she broke from her sobbing convulsions, Elena looked distant. Dark circles drug her eyelids down, and her voice was shaken as she relived the memory of the day. "They saw it."

"Who?"

"You had already gone. Ran off with a shadow hound chasing you. But me and the others, we were still in the amusement park. I kept running in circles as they raced around us. Their galloping was so loud, it disoriented us. I fell into a basket of my roses. The thorns dug into my skin, but I didn't even notice. I was scared to death and full of adrenaline. I held them in my hands, two stems, waving them around. And they saw it. The other villagers saw that the shadow hounds avoided me."

"Elena . . ."

"They begged me," she chirped, then choked on a cough. "They saw it and they knew it would save them. But I just watched them and cried. My arms were frozen. I did nothing. And now, all of them . . . just gone. They're all dead, and I could have saved them. Some of them. Any of them." Elena looked at him, her face a statue of depression and sadness. "But I didn't."

This time, Alex stared down at the blanket. All the words he could have offered, all the comfort of the world he wished to offer, were stuck in his throat. Uselessly, he repeated her name, feeling impotent with his inability to solve their crisis.

"I understand loss, Sasha. I understand the pain, and the confusion, of knowing that something you did to save yourself cost someone else their life."

"But will they understand it?" he asked weakly. "If I tell

them about zhar-ptysia, will they pardon me with the same empathy you feel?"

"No," she answered honestly, flatly, as she watched him. "I was wrong. You should not tell them."

"Will you keep my secret?"

She nodded, hugging her arms around him as she suddenly dove forward. "Even if you told them mine."

Alex wrapped his arms around her, and her touch lingered. Their bodies heated with the passion of their sadness and their regret, but perhaps also from their mutual understanding and admiration. Elena's eyes lingered on his for some time as she watched the starlight twinkle in them. When they finally broke their affectionate stare, it was into the embrace of their locked lips.

Pushing him onto his back, Elena fell against his chest, holding him dearly close. "This could be the last night we have, Sasha. Any of us."

"Don't talk like that," he insisted.

"Every day could be your last, no? Tomorrow just seems

more likely than other days have before."

"Elena—"

She interrupted him with a finger on his lips. "Do not go to sleep with regrets, nor promises you can't keep, Sasha. Kiss me like the first time you met me, and as though it will be the last time you will. And if this is to be our last night together, make love to me like you could stay with me forever."

Alex stared up at her, a soft pain in his chest that appeared and lingered every time he saw her face. There was a fondness that existed between them that he had not felt in years, that he missed more than each breath he puffed in and out of his lungs. He swore he would never love again, but here, in this moment, he felt as though he had come home to her. And that realization sent his eyes wide.

"K-Katya . . . ?"

"Just kiss me," she whispered, and they lost themselves in each other.

*

The earth exhaled with a deep, gluttonous groan. A quake followed that chopped the waters of the river into bouncing laps as though fish were leaping out from beneath the surface. Alex awoke in a daze, rubbing at his eyes as he tried to orient himself in the midst of the tumultuous panic that was erupting.

It was early in the morning, day of the festival, 26 April. Alex hurriedly dressed himself beneath the blanket that coated him. His skin shivered in the night air as the ground continued to shake. He was alone.

His mind swam over his time with Elena. A fog clamped down on his memories like a migraine. He fought to remember the details, but they were fading rapidly, though it was more obvious this time than before. Some force, some oddity, was purposefully preventing him from recalling these events, or any event since he came to this place.

In the distance, there was a light beaconing out of Chernobyl like a lighthouse tower. Alex squinted as he focused on it. It had been there all this time, but somehow he'd failed to notice the nuclear monolith even during his time in Pripyat the day prior.

Alex rubbed his temples. Chernobyl stirred more memories that he couldn't reach. Was this truly the first time he'd seen it? The structure was so huge, and so powerful. He felt intimidated by it, even afraid of it, but he didn't remember why.

The light shone unwavering from Chernobyl into Pripyat. While mostly white, there were shreds and streaks of gold beaming through the column. It reminded him of something he'd seen when the shadow hounds interrupted the festival preparations.

"Elena!" he called out, the idea of those roaming monsters giving him great apprehension. Alex nervously looked out over the high grass that sat along the riverbank. Something stirred nearby, out of sight. "Elena, is that you?"

There was no response, but the rustling grew closer. Alex backed away slightly, but the water of the river was right at his heels. He would feel no safer in the sluggishness of the mud and tide if an attack were upon him.

Holding up his hands, Alex braced himself. Whatever had been moving in the brush was now close. He tensed and held his breath. The movement stopped, which worsened his anxiety. Seconds ticked by without a sound. Exhaling sharply, Alex gasped as he realized the two rose stems were still lying on the blanket. But as he shifted to reach for them, the grass split and the underside of a spade cracked across his head.

Alex rolled around in the dirt, mumbling as his vision blurred. Another smack of the shovel vibrated off his skull, making him near motionless. His eyes hung open drunkenly, then slipped closed.

There was scraping, clumping, and grunting sounds emanating around him. He couldn't focus. The pain was incredible and it kept him held down, causing him to slip in and out of consciousness.

When his eyes opened again, his body slid a short distance, then sailed downward. His back bounced on marshy ground with a splash that bubbled up from beneath him. He was lying in a hole.

A grave.

There was a figure, a man, who stood looming over him at the top of the hole. The man lingered only a moment before digging the shovel into the muddy dirt and throwing a pile toppling down onto Alex.

"I will save them, by God I will," the priest said, working hurriedly to bury the evidence of the boy's sin. "You have brought hell with you, but I will send it back with your soul. God have mercy on me, but these hounds of hell will claim no others, either through their actions or yours, demon!"

Fingers twitching, Alex weakly tried to reach up to him, to plead with him in the hopes that he would alter this irrational course of action. But a clump of mud smacked over his face. His head bounced. He began to choke and smother on the thick, wet soil, until all he could feel was the weight of it pushing him down.

Chapter Eight

The woodsman stood with his rifle clutched in his right hand, a rose prominently displayed on his chest with early morning dew still coating it. With the sun barely rendering the sky in faint pastel blues and pinks, it was a surprise to him that so many people were awake—even more so that they were rowdy and readying themselves for war.

Pacing around near him was Dmitriy, the woodsman's apprentice. An axe hung in a sling on his back, two pistols sat in holsters on his hips, and a rifle was firmly in his grip.

"That's a bit much, isn't it?" the old hunter asked.

Dmitriy looked himself over slowly, then lifted his rifle to his chest as though he were a soldier on display. "Do you not think I'm ready?"

"Didn't say that," he replied with a grunt. "Just looks heavy."

"And tell me, my mentor, how does one arm themselves to fight the devil and his dog army?"

Groaning angrily, the woodsman shoved the smaller man in the chest, sending him toppling down into the dirt. "Not this again!"

Weakly pushing himself up onto his elbows, Dmitriy struggled to his feet. The axe on his back felt like an anchor, but he would never admit it. "I'm not saying anything the others aren't thinking."

"And what do you think speaking like this will do to their morale, boy?" the woodsman asked with a growl in his throat. "I don't care what you all think, but I care that you don't think it right now. I need you strong, all of you."

Dmitriy glanced at the dirt with his imprint and kicked his boot over it to cover his fall. "I'm not as brave as you, Woodsman."

The woodsman's large hands adjusted his apprentice's clothes and twisted the stem of the rose on his chest to secure it. "You don't need to be. You just need aim." Setting him down, the man fished a pipe and some matches from a pack on his waist. "So don't drop your rifle. And if you drop that, don't drop your pistols. And if you drop *those*, then for God's sake don't drop your axe."

"And if I drop that?" the young man asked with a smile.

The gesture was returned in kind as the old hunter lit his pipe and puffed. "Then don't drop your pants as you flee, or you will be remembered poorly, Dmitriy."

More men gathered as the haze of morning began to clear and the sun rose higher. There was no organization to the crowd. Some wore makeshift armors of thick leather that looked to be strewn together from farming gear. Several men had taken their oven doors as chest guards secured with rope.

This was no army, no fighting force—this was life, simple life, gathering to preserve itself.

"How go your preparations?" asked an approaching man.

Turning to face the priest, the woodsman's stare reminded him of their disdain for one another. "The men are courageous, even in their fear. There are not enough rifles for the village, barely enough for half, and so the rest have brought their shovels, their rakes, and their axes."

"We are a rabble."

"We are a *village*," the woodsman corrected him. "I don't have time to train these people to be an army, and most of them don't have a fighting spirit even if I did. But they will defend their home, because they must."

Focusing on the woodsman's chest, and the rose pinned upon it, the priest scowled. "I see you chose to put your faith in superstition rather than the more appropriate choice."

The woodsman adjusted his rose slightly, staring at it for a moment as he contemplated. "Did it ever occur to you that God has given us a means to defend ourselves?"

"Not when the salvation came from the mouth of the

demon that brought these things to us," the priest countered with venom in his voice.

"You don't know that. And you never gave him a chance. I spent time with Alex, and I don't believe it's anything more than coincidence. To me, it's just as likely that God sent him here to help us face the shadow hounds."

The priest threw his arms out to the side and paced in a wide circle. "Then where is he? Where is your deliverer? Does he not ride with you, a rose pinned to his chest as well? You would march against hell with a flower as your armor, and he is tardy to the fray?"

Huffing, the woodsman tapped the remains of his pipe onto the ground and returned it to his satchel. Begrudgingly, there was some truth to those words. "Find Elena. Surely, she must know where he is."

Dmitriy shook his head, up until now playing the part of a silent bystander. "She's not at home, Woodsman. We've been picking roses from her garden all morning. The house is empty."

He sighed heavily, swinging his arms as if boxing his frustration. "We have no idea when the shadow hounds could strike, so we don't have the time or the men to waste looking for them."

"Do you see now?" the priest asked, a knowing glint in his eyes. "Abandon this foolishness and put your faith back where it belongs."

Glaring at him with wild eyes, the woodsman brushed the man aside and off-balance as he strode toward the awaiting men. "Then you will march with us, Priest, to show us the proper way."

The priest stared at him with wide eyes soaked with nervousness. Dmitriy stepped toward the holy man and held out a rose stem.

"You might want to bring this with you, sir," he offered. "Just in case."

Angrily smacking the flower to the ground, the priest scared the apprentice off after his master. But as he lingered, staring down at the rose, he hesitated.

With all the men assembled, the woodsman called them

all close. They huddled inward, watching him.

"I'm not one for speeches," he admitted. "I hunt beasts and I feed you their meat. These creatures, though we've given them powerful names, are nothing more than beasts. We are going to hunt them, and we are going to kill them."

"Is it true you shot one before?" asked a villager, hoping for some kind of anecdote.

The woodsman nodded. "I did, in the Wormwood Forest. I shot it, but it lives."

"Then how do we defeat them, sir?"

"We shoot it more," he replied, thankful to hear some chuckles among them. "Be mindful of your brothers when you aim your rifles. You kneel down to reload so the men behind you can fire. I see steel in some of your hands. I want you protecting our flanks so they don't swallow our sides. We move together, we stay together. Do not run. Do not die. And whoever kills the first one will have a hero's feast in their honor. I will personally cater to them the finest meal we have ever known."

The men cheered, pumping their weapons into the air. Together they began to march, the woodsman boldly leading the charge. Unsurprising to him, the priest dawdled at the rear.

Before they cleared the town perimeter, a woman came running off the doorstep and into the crowd, shaking at her husband. "The domovyk! He is gone! How could he leave us at a time like this?"

The husband fought with her prying hands, trying to remain focused on the upcoming fight. "It does not matter! We will ask him to come home later!"

"But who will look after me while you're away?"

Stepping in on the villager's behalf, the woodsman grunted at her. "We are all looking after you, woman. If you wish for us to stay, we can await the shadow hounds in your home. Otherwise, let us ride and kill these damn things so your domovyk may come home with nothing to fear."

There was a short cheer from the men and their pace increased, adrenaline fueling them as much as fear. The wife stopped and watched them slip away toward Chernobyl.

A stern look sat uncomfortably on the woodsman's face as they continued on. "Why would it leave?" he murmured to himself.

*

Clawing and scraping, his hands fought against the dirt that packed him down. Alex could feel the tears in his skin, the peeling of his nails, and the nothingness as the air left his lungs.

Then it happened again.

His body convulsed and he jumped upward, fighting to free himself until he found his head swimming in euphoria. The world went black until there was nothing. No sound, no light.

But then it all came back.

Alex strained, pushing his hand up as far as it would go. It felt warmer than the dark, wet earth that entombed him. Was it sunlight? Had he made it?

Unexpectedly, something reached out and took his hand. Alex panicked, wishing he could recoil and keep himself hidden, but the bliss was starting to steal his mind again. He clenched his eyes tight and pulled, and to his surprise, the gripping hand pulled as well.

Rising from the earth with a heavy gasp into free air, Alex choked and rolled on the surface. Water and mud poured out of his mouth as he retched, eventually giving way to coughing and panting as he adjusted to the influx of air in his lungs.

His eyes were wild and having trouble adjusting to the world around him. "Who's there?" he asked, but there was no response.

Fear reminded him of the last time he sat in this same spot, calling out with nothing in return. The priest's voice was still in his ears, spouting his rationale for such an atrocious act. Somehow, Alex couldn't bring himself to blame the man. If this new world had been so confusing to him, he could only imagine how the others must have reacted to his arrival, the shadow hounds, and the deaths. He was a scapegoat. Or, in the worst of all his fears, he may have even been responsible.

Alex took his time until the details formed in his eyes. He first stared down at his hands, which were pressed into the ground to hold him up. They were flawless. He saw none of the blood or damage he expected, but he was positive he had not imagined his struggle. Just as he was positive he had drowned, numerous times, in that hole.

"I understand now," he whispered, smiling faintly as he felt the cloud lifting from his mind. "Whatever he was trying to do, he set me free. I remember . . . *everything*."

When he sat back, he leveled his gaze and was surprised at the group that gathered there. At least a dozen berehyni floated in the air, staring cautiously back at him. Behind and all around them was another curious and strange set of creatures, and double in number.

The second group all seemed related in some way. They were not unlike people; in fact, they were structurally identical to humans, but admittedly more grotesque in appearance. All of them were abundantly hairy, in most cases covering their entire bodies like some kind of Sasquatch.

One of them sat in the sand, its arms and legs soppy with water. It heaved a large exhale, looking over to Alex and giving him an affectionate—if not powerful—shove. The force toppled him over, mostly to the amusement of the other creatures.

Looking past the jokester, Alex recognized one of their kind standing away from the gathered group. It glanced over at him repeatedly, its eyes darting away just as quickly. Standing there with a shovel in its meaty paw, it focused down on it as if to distract its gaze.

Alex recognized the shovel from Elena's rose garden. He had used it when helping to prepare for the festival.

"I remember you, too," Alex said to it, clearing his throat with another cough. "I saw you when I left for Pripyat. You're her domovyk, aren't you? The pots banging?"

Its gaze continued to shift about, but it nodded.

"You're all domovye." Alex found the strength to rise up to his feet, offering a hand to the seated one that had pulled him free. It took the offering and stood much higher than him, droplets trickling from its scraggly hair. "Why are you here? And where's Elena?"

None of them replied. Their gazes shifted to one another as though they were discussing the idea among themselves.

With minor frustration, Alex conceded that he was having a one-way conversation. "Okay, fine. Where is Katya, then?" Her domovyk shot a stare in his direction, this time lingering on him without shyness. The name felt strange on his tongue, only because it was so obviously familiar that he had no idea why it had taken him so long to remember it. "Katya, domovyk. Where is she?"

Angrily, it stomped like a troll into the mud. Heavy paw imprints remained as it marched around, shaking the shovel into the air and hooting wildly.

Impatiently, Alex walked toward it. "I asked you a question. Where—" he began, but was interrupted by the berehynia that darted into his face. He watched the tiny creature closely, which peered at him with a tiresome frown. Slowly, the little thing turned and pointed off into the distance. Alex followed the horizon until his eyes landed on Chernobyl.

"And the villagers? The shadow hounds?"

Again, the berehynia aimed in the same direction.

"What can I do?" he asked, his voice choked by his indulgence in his self-doubt and woe. Alex paused when another berehynia flew up to him, a rose in its hands. It offered the flower to him. "You want me to fight the shadow hounds?"

It nodded, gesturing the rose at him again.

Reluctantly, he took it from the berehynia with an unsteady hand. "You all understand this world. You all *are* this world. So please, tell me . . . is all of this is happening because of me?" None of them replied, nodded, or otherwise gestured. Their silence only solidified the notion in his mind. "Oh my God, it's true. The priest was right. This is my fault."

But several berehyni were in his face, waving their

scolding fingers at him. They wore such strict expressions that it actually brought a small smile to Alex's face. Their insistence was convincing.

"Okay, but how can I fight them alone? What can I do?"

At that moment, all the creatures—domovye and berehyni—approached him, straightening their postures and assembling in two rows. They waited.

Alex looked out over them all. "You'll fight with me?"

In unison, they nodded. Katya's domovyk approached Alex and pushed the shovel into his hands. He stumbled backward and stared at it, chuckling at its simplicity. It was a foolish thing to think he would bring a garden tool to war. But something else was nagging at his heart, beckoning his attention.

With a strange compulsion, Alex fished around his pockets, checking them all until his palm clutched the small burlap sack he'd tucked away. It pulsated like a heartbeat as he held it, and upon opening it the light exploded.

Shielding his eyes, Alex held the feather out away from

himself like a torch with too much heat. He heard the cry in the sky. Zhar-ptysia dove down into him like a comet, exploding outward and flattening him into the dirt. The creatures scattered for cover as dirt rained down from the sky and the river water rippled violently.

When the dust settled, Alex emerged uninjured. Slowly, the creatures stalked back to him, awestruck. He stood at the ready, holding a sword of fire in his right hand in place of the shovel. Twirling it about, it felt natural. Somehow, he knew how to wield it.

Alex looked out over his makeshift army with a passion burning as strongly in his eyes as the lick of flame on his blade. "So be it, friends. Let's go to war." He stepped past the domovye and berehyni. Chernobyl was squarely in his sights as he advanced. "I'm coming, Katya."

The line of creatures charged after him, as if to proclaim in harmonious agreement: 'to war.'

Chapter Nine

The lighthouse beam fired from Chernobyl into Pripyat at a constant rate. As pure as the driven snow, the bright column was nearly blinding, but the severity was occasionally broken by the streaks of gold shooting through it.

Leading the villagers toward the monolith, the woodsman raised his arm into the air to halt them once they reached what he considered to be a safe distance. He watched the structure nervously as if he had a reason to fear it etched somewhere in the back of his mind. Indeed, the very fact that he could not remember such a structure ever existed was baffling. Surely it had been there all along.

As expected, the sky began to darken. For a few moments, the beacon emanating from the reactor was overwhelmingly bright, but it too began to fade. Crackles of orange and red churned through it like flames, until suddenly they began to strike like bolts of lightning into the ground.

With tiny explosions, the shadow hounds began to rise up out of the earth, their filthy bodies carrying all the rot and ruin of nightmare. Their eyes flickered red, as if igniting. Two, four, six . . . their numbers multiplied rapidly with more sparks launching out every few seconds.

Dropping down to his knee, the woodsman roared as he squeezed back the trigger of his rifle, "Fire!"

Bullets whisked forward, impacting the shadow hounds with dull, unsatisfying thumps. Patches of maggot-clustered dirt fell from their hulking bodies as they charged at the villagers. The men were overcome with fear at the sight of the beasts, but impressively, they held their footing.

The roses shimmered in unison, like a pulse, and the shadow hounds slowed, then stopped entirely before the group. They circled the men, chomping at the bit but somehow unable to close the distance.

Dmitriy reloaded his rifle quickly as he watched one of the beasts move past him. "The roses—it's true! They hesitate!"

The man beside him cheered, lowering his rake for a moment as he celebrated his joy. But the shadow hound snapped forward, its jaws taking hold of his ankle and clamping down. With a rapid jerk of its head, the beast tossed the villager like a discarded doll.

Landing harshly, the man felt the breath leave his lungs on impact. He cried out, reaching down to his leg where the monster had bit him. The skin turned black before it crumbled away like ash. Screaming, he rolled about as the infection spread. His rose curled up into a sickly ball and wilted as the man faded to dust beneath it.

"Don't let them touch you!" the woodsman warned,

smashing the butt of his rifle down onto the head of the closest circling beast before turning it about and firing into it.

"Close the gap!" Dmitriy added, shuffling closer to the next man at his side.

A rifleman fell next, then two more flank defenders. The villagers began to panic. Even the woodsman was losing his confidence. At the rear of the line, the priest trembled. He babbled prayers loosely, their verses all running together in his mind.

With no illusions of hope remaining, the priest turned and began to run. Dmitriy called after him, firing out at the beast that took pursuit before another pounced on top of him. Dmitriy shoved the barrel of his rifle into its mouth, trying to keep it at bay.

The priest panted as he ran, begging loudly as the shadow hound approached. Turning, he fished a rose out of his pocket and threw it at the monster, which jumped easily over it and smacked a heavy paw into the priest, sending him rolling. The priest reached his hands up into the air and shouted as he backed away.

Offering neither ceremony nor delay, the shadow hound leapt forward, but met with unexpected resistance. Three domovye tackled it at that instant and ran back with it in their clutches. When they drove it to the ground, they pummeled its body with their meaty fists until there was nothing left but a pile of dirt.

Alex ran toward the villagers, swinging his sword in wide arcs to scare away a pair of the beasts before driving it deep into the body of the one pinning Dmitriy. He kept his pace for a few moments before thrusting outward, tossing the shadow hound's body forward. It ignited into flame as it sailed to the ground.

Pivoting quickly, Alex swung his sword straight out, unleashing a furious column of fire into another monster. Dmitriy rolled to his feet, tossing his rifle aside as he drew his pistols from his belt.

"Help them!" he called to the men to rally their spirits. Leveling his pistols, be began to fire anew. "Help Sasha!

God help us all!"

With a bayonet affixed to his rifle, the woodsman lunged forward in attack, piercing the body of the beast before him. It bucked wildly, and to his surprise, the blade broke off inside its horrible body. The move caught him off balance, and the woodsman landed on his rear.

Quickly drawing another knife, he prepared to defend himself until he saw no further need. The berehyni swooped in angrily. Their fingers were poised like daggers, their teeth bared like fangs as they dove into the body of the beast, tearing it apart piece by piece until nothing remained.

"Thank you, little fireflies!" the woodsman barked, rising back into the fight.

Alex struck down another shadow hound with a furious carving slash, swiveling to face another. He swung again, but the beast darted like a lightning bolt. Its entire body was a blur, suddenly intangible as it danced across the ground rapidly with unnatural speed. It was retreating.

They all were. Every remaining beast exited the fight and sailed backward toward the beacon. There was a moment of celebration, but it was quickly broken by the massive tremor that threw every man and creature from their feet.

The image of Chernobyl seemed to twist around before them. Alex pushed his sword into the ground for leverage, rising back to a fighting stance as he readied himself. There was a flash, as if reality itself pulsated, and then a final punch into the earth.

Then, it was there. Another shadow hound, but larger, at least five times larger than the rest. It stood towering above its pack, digging its claws into the ground, which curled into scorched pockets of death beneath its mighty hooves. This was their leader. This was the Lord of the Shadow Hounds.

"Cleanse," it bellowed, the very word causing the air to ripple against Alex's flesh.

"Cleanse!" the pack chanted in response.

"They speak!" the woodsman gasped.

"As if they weren't fearsome enough," Dmitriy added.

Alex narrowed his eyes and raised his sword, aiming it at the abomination. "I want Katya!"

It snarled back at him, clawing at the ground as it readied to advance. Bravely, Alex took the first step and they charged at one another. Each gallop of the massive beast caused earthquakes. The villagers were frozen a short distance away, bouncing under the pressure of the tremors, helpless to watch events unfold.

Alex swung out and dashed to the left, his fiery blade striking at the mouth of the monster. But the Lord of the Shadow Hounds bit down and tore in the opposite direction. The sword shattered with a small explosion, broken as though it were nothing but a twig. Hot flames swirled in the monster's mouth like lava as it exhaled smoke from its nostrils.

Alex landed in a stumble and toppled over. His sword was gone, and his hand dropped the broken wooden shovel that remained as he cried out, "Zhar-ptysia!"

The Lord of the Shadow Hounds chewed harshly, spewing fire from its mouth until it faded. Only darkness remained. The berehyni and domovye hesitated, along with the villagers, keeping their distance to avoid provoking the mighty beast. Slowly, it turned to face Alex again, staring down at him with intense hatred.

"I-I know she's here," he stammered, gazing up into the face of his would-be executioner. "Please."

The monster lingered over him, unwavering, before it finally turned away and marched back toward its pack. "No."

"Please!" Alex shouted, jumping up. "I remember now! I understand what's happening! You have to—"

"You understand nothing!" it roared as it snapped its head back in his direction. "She came to us willingly, to fix what was broken, and so it shall be. By the time your Festival of Lights ends, this will be over. Return to your village, all of you, and you will never again know of this wretchedness."

"I . . . I died," he said, the words sounding strange and foolish in his ears. "The priest buried me alive, and I died. Over and over again. But here I am, still standing here. I know this is my fault, okay? It's my fault, not hers."

"You did not die. Not yet." The Lord of the Shadow Hounds turned halfway to face him again. "This world is broken, but you did not break it. You are a casualty, not a catalyst."

Confusion swept his face as he wiped the tears from his eyes. The beast was correct; he truly did not understand.

The woodsman approached Alex cautiously, putting his hand on the boy's shoulder as he watched the Lord of the Shadow Hounds. "No more bloodshed?" he asked the beast.

"No more," it agreed.

"And this will all be over by the end of the festival?"

"It is already over, if you simply turn away."

Alex shook his head. "No. That's not acceptable. I want to see her! Please, bring me to Katya."

But the Lord of the Shadow Hounds was resistant. "You may never gain the clarity you seek. But soon, you will not remember clarity, nor will you ever see or remember her face again. At the close of this festival, the wrongs will be righted, and she will be gone."

"Then take me as well!" Alex cried, fully familiar with

the sensation it had described. It was the cloud that had suppressed him ever since he awoke in the village—something that kept his memories beyond his reach, and the thought of her memory being lost as well was too much for him to bear.

"Sasha, no!" the woodsman interjected, but Alex pushed him aside.

"Take me!" he repeated.

Growling, the Lord of the Shadow Hounds turned away, retreating back toward Chernobyl. "Return to the place where it began. You will find understanding there. Then you will know what cannot be."

The woodsman looked worried. "What's there?"

It paused for only a second, giving them a final look. "He is there, with the last decision he will ever make."

The Shadow Hounds faded away as the sky cleared. Daylight was still upon them, and the beacon of light continued to pour uninterrupted from Chernobyl to Pripyat. The villagers quietly rose from the ground, checking on one another. The domovye and berehyni returned to the village with their shoulders slouched, defeat weighing them down as they moved slowly through the mud of the battleground.

After several minutes of deep breaths, Alex steadied himself, raising his gaze to the woodsman's eyes. "Please take me there. Take me where it all began."

"Alex, I—"

"My memories . . . I already feel it. This place is trying to steal them from me. I can't lose them again. I can't lose *her* again. Please, Woodsman." The resolve in Alex's eyes was clear, as was his duty.

"Very well." The woodsman turned and looked out toward the line of trees nearby. "We go to the Wormwood Forest."

Chapter Ten

The trees of the Wormwood Forest flickered like flashbulbs, their appearance changing rapidly. They were green, then red. Barren, then cast aflame. The cycle repeated as though it were an orchestrated illusion of seasons and demise, coruscating like a violent storm.

Alex dully stepped forward, all the questions and doubt from his previous encounter causing his feet to drag. Reality itself seemed confused the deeper they moved into the forest.

Behind him, the woodsman walked in circles, his eyes lingering on the changing scenery. It was speaking to him somehow, or dredging up something buried within him.

"This is right," he said, tilting his head around. "Or it isn't. Damn it, none of this makes sense."

"No," Alex agreed. "Or maybe it does."

The woodsman grunted at him. "Are you mocking me?"

"No more than the world mocks us both." His sarcasm was as lame as his footing. "How much farther?"

"I don't know."

"You what?"

"I don't know!" the woodsman repeated. "Nothing looks right here. None of this is the same. It keeps changing!"

Alex turned to him with disbelieving eyes. "Are you telling me you're afraid of some trees?"

The woodsman recoiled, releasing an awkward guffaw. "You must be mad."

"Then you want me to believe the village's greatest tracker can't tell me where he found me?"

Another rush of flame warmed the air around them

before it disappeared. The old hunter ducked down and cursed as he circled again. "This damn forest!"

"What the hell is the matter with you, Woodsman?"

"My brother *died* in this forest!" he shouted, then backed away with a hand clamped to his mouth. His eyes were wide and filled with incredulity. "Why would I say that? I don't know that. How could I know that? Oh my God, my brother, where are you?"

Frowning, Alex looked away, trying to determine his path at random. "You should go."

But the woodsman was now on his knees, rocking back and forth and holding his head as if to prevent his thoughts from leaking. "Moi brat!" he cried in his native tongue. "Moi brat!"

Alex grabbed him by his shirt and shook him. "You are the lisovyk!" he shouted. The woodsman smacked at him, trying to push him away, but Alex persisted. "You are the lisovyk, Woodsman!"

"Lisovyk," he repeated weakly.

"Lisovyk," Alex said, nodding. "This is your brother's forest. You have to pull yourself together."

"Lisovyk," the woodsman said again, though with greater understanding in his voice. Around them, the trees shifted to flame, but this time held their appearance. He rose to his feet. "My brother was . . . the lisovyk. Here. In the forest."

Turning around, Alex worriedly watched the flames, though he felt no heat. "What's happening, Woodsman?"

The trees twisted and groaned as though they were alive, dying as they bent and lurched in every direction. Alex smelled burning pine as the trunks of the trees were stained crimson. They shriveled thinly, their branches reaching out like frail, elderly creatures.

"This isn't Wormwood Forest, not anymore," the woodsman acknowledged, his voice crisper. "This is the Red Forest now. The radiation flooded the land. Killed it all. My brother, the lisovyk . . . he died here. He died so many years ago. Of course he did. When the reactor failed, he died with the forest."

"Chernobyl," Alex concluded, the name holding more recognition in his mind with each passing second. "The reactor exploded. There were helicopters."

"And firemen," the woodsman added with a faint smile. "Sasha, I am sorry. It seems I misled you. The things I remembered, the way I put it together. It was—"

"It's not your fault."

"I feel like such a fool." He placed his hands into the soil. "All this time, pining after the idea that he was still alive. When really, he's been gone for"—he paused, sniffing the air—"decades. Oh my God, is that right?"

Alex knelt down beside him. His mind was awash as the cloud fought to regain control of him, but he nodded. "Yeah, I think so. It's been a long time."

Rising up, the woodsman dusted his hands off on his clothes. He smiled again, his expression a peculiar mix of depression and appreciation. "Thank you, Sasha. I don't know if I ever would have realized that without you."

Alex frowned at the old hunter, patting him on the arm.

"I just hope you can hold onto that memory. It's been so hard keeping my mind intact lately."

The woodsman reached forward and pulled the man into a hug, patting his back fondly. "Come, Sasha. Let us find you the same peace of mind."

They continued on together with a greater sense of direction. With the woodsman's head now clear, he knew where they were going. They walked more briskly, even though the anticipation was building in Alex's chest.

Despite reality cooperating behind them, there were ripples of static ahead, near a paved road. A sound echoed repeatedly, and it was something he recognized. A buzzing, a whirling that hummed through the air in slow motion.

A wheel.

Alex looked beneath his boot, lifting it from the ground. The wheel of the motorcycle was bent there, covered in roots and dirt that tugged it downward, burying it out of sight and mind.

"My memories," Alex declared aloud, leaning over to brush his fingertips across the wheel. "They're here."

Stepping toward him, the woodsman put a hand on his shoulder. "I think I tried to tell you before, Sasha, but . . . so are you."

It was as if a window had opened before them. There was a fog that hovered in the shape of an oval. Images flickered across it like a projector coming to life. It became translucent, and Alex's eyes widened slowly as he stared through the looking glass.

The motorcycle was smashed into the ground on the edge of the forest. It was a gnarled, mangled mess, mostly from the helpless roll forward into the tree line. Alex saw himself there, surrounded by men in military and paramedic uniforms.

He watched them pick up his body and place it on a stretcher, which they hurried up the short ditch onto the road and then into the back of an ambulance. His body bounced softly as they moved him, as though he were on the back of a rolling wooden cart.

Alex stared into his own eyes as they rolled around the

back of the ambulance. They found Chernobyl in the distance, then they faded to black. The paramedics reached for a pair of paddles and placed them on his chest.

His body jumped on the stretcher, and he gasped loudly. The image—the very world—froze. Watching himself laying there, Alex's eyes filled with pain, his face twisting. "I saw her," he admitted as he turned to the woodsman. "In front of my motorcycle that night. I saw Katya."

"Yes," groaned a heavy voice as the ground shifted in their wake. The Lord of the Shadow Hounds rose into view, approaching them slowly. Somehow, his heavy footfalls were very nearly muted. Perhaps it was because of this, or the sincerity of his prior promises, but they were not afraid of his presence. "You are remembering now."

The woodsman steadied Alex as the boy tried to cope with the images. "Go on, boy. Finish it."

"And . . . and I . . . I tried to avoid her, and . . ." He looked between the two of them. "I crashed."

"Why was she here?" the woodsman asked.

"She does not know," the Lord of the Shadow Hounds

replied. "She cannot know. It was mere compulsion. Somewhere in the endless sea of improbability, she found the one thing that would change the tide."

Alex looked at the beast. "It was me. She was looking for me."

"Yes."

"She knew I'd be here."

"Compulsion," it agreed. "And she found you, although in doing so she tore open the space between and brought you here. She was the catalyst. You were simply a casualty, like I said."

The woodsman looked to the Lord of the Shadow Hounds. "What about all the people we lost? What about those victims?"

"All will be made right," it promised. "They will awake in their beds. None of you will remember this trauma. You will have your peace."

Alex pointed at the ambulance and his fallen body. "So what happens to me?"

"That is your final decision."

He looked back through the window to the other side. "This place is . . . is this death?"

The Lord of the Shadow Hounds bared its teeth in a knowing smile. "There is no death, only what comes next. For her, this was the place to find peace. But whether you would find peace here is not for me to decide."

"It's for me," Alex whispered, his eyes fixated on himself. "But you're still taking her? I won't remember her?"

"To close the gap, we require her sacrifice. By the end of the festival, it will be done. No one here will remember her." The beast turned its cold red eyes to the woodsman. "I cannot say you will remember your brother either, lisovyk. You will remember hope, but that hope will be stained with doubt."

The woodsman grunted. "I'd rather live with hope than the insanity of uncertainty."

"As you wish," it bellowed, bowing its head with respect.

"But if I go back," Alex began, "then I will remember her?"

The beast nodded. "Nothing governs your life or memory on that side but you. Here, things are preserved, along with any memories that threaten the balance. It is not malicious. It is merely to bring you the peace you have earned—the peace you have chosen. You know what your life will be here. There, you will live for as long as you will, remembering what you will. You may mourn, live, and love as you please. But you will not remember this place any more than the dream it was for you. That is your choice."

"To live or die, here or there," Alex murmured, barely able to stand against the gravity of the situation.

"You would be missed," the woodsman offered. "But I cannot keep you from your heart."

"I know peace here," he admitted. "And love. But what are those things if I can't have them with her?" Alex stared at the ambulance for a long time. Sadness overwhelmed him. "I can't lose her again."

Turning away, the Lord of the Shadow Hounds departed. With a confident nod, the woodsman lifted his hand in parting and turned away as well.

"Good-bye, Sasha," he said quietly.

Alex closed his eyes, tears squeezing through. The gap between worlds rippled and cracked as time began to bleed back into the features.

"Never again," he whispered.

Shattering, the window vanished. The doors slammed shut on the back of the ambulance. It reanimated and sped forward, leaving the crash in its wake.

Chapter Eleven

As the light beamed into Pripyat from Chernobyl, the streaks of gold mixed into the beacon broke off and took life of their own. At times, they assumed the shape of a family walking the streets together. Some formed objects like benches, parked vehicles, and other flashes of memory from a time since past.

Katya stood on the edge of the city and looked on at these snapshots of life from long ago—of a time when she was a child in Pripyat. The Lord of the Shadow Hounds approached her.

"I'm in there, somewhere, you know," she mentioned, keeping her eyes fixed ahead. "Right now, some ribbon of light is painting footsteps I was too young to remember, or some snack in the pantry I never ate."

The beast stopped short of her, lowering its head in reverence. "I will not disturb your final moments more than to remind you of your duty. You must not return to the village, nor speak with anyone. And when the time comes, at the end of your Festival of Lights, you will cross over into peace."

"Tomorrow afternoon," she said. "When the evacuation began."

"You do not suffer the burdens of memory loss any longer, I see." She did not respond, and the Lord of the Shadow Hounds lingered. "It must be difficult not to say good-bye to your people. I admire your selflessness."

She shrugged dismissively. "I already said good-bye to the one who mattered most. It was beautiful, and I will cherish that memory for as long as I can have it. You know, just for a second before this place choked it from him, he even remembered that it was—"

Katya gasped as she turned, her hand clamping over her mouth. Stepping past the Lord of the Shadow Hounds, Alex smiled even as the tears fell down her cheeks.

"Elena was your grandmother's name," he said as he reached for her. "You have an old soul, right? That thing that drew you back here, that notion, was from that phrase. I remember when you told me, lying in that hospital bed. It's been you, Katya. It's been you this entire time."

"You really did come to visit," she said as she leapt forward, burying herself in his arms. They openly wept together. She stepped back from him, pawing at him in shocked disbelief. "How . . . ?"

"I made my decision," he said, sparing a glance to the beast beside them. "I'm here now. I crossed over completely."

The words would have been foreign to anyone else, but she knew exactly what he meant. She was horrified. "No! You cannot, Sasha. You can't! You have to live!"

"Not without you. Never again without you."

"B-but . . . " She looked to the Lord of the Shadow Hounds. "How can he . . . ?"

It nodded. "You will cross together, tomorrow, when the festival ends."

"But we don't know what happens next. We could be gone, we could be lost, we could—"

Alex shushed her. "We could live together forever. You're right, we don't know what's next, but it's worth it, Katya. It's worth finding out with you. Even if it's just one more night, it's a night we didn't have before. And I'd like to spend it with you as though we'll never have another one."

A smile spread over her lips. Katya understood his reference to their last night together. "I wanted to tell you, but the longer we were together, the more I started to believe the dream again. But I knew it wasn't real. Ever since I caused you to . . ." She frowned. "Ever since I started all of this suffering, I knew it wasn't a dream. It was a nightmare. A forced smile. A lie."

"It's still their dream, Katya." Alex reached down and

took her hand in his. "And this is ours now, for as long as it lasts."

"Until tomorrow," she agreed. "And every day after. I love you, Sasha."

"I love you, Katya."

The Lord of the Shadow Hounds exhaled and turned from them. "Your fates are intertwined completely now, but your evening is none of my concern." It began its march back toward Chernobyl.

Alex shed a grin for the beast. "Good night, shadow hound. We will see you tomorrow."

"No, Alex," it said, its body crumbling to dust and sifting off into the wind. "You will never see me again."

Placing a kiss on his lips, Katya kept her arms wrapped around him without any intention of letting go. "How would you like to see my home when I was a child?"

His expression brightened. "Okay, but I also want to ride the Ferris wheel with you."

"Tomorrow," she promised.

Alex and Katya felt the warm glow of gold overtake their bodies as they sauntered off into the living tapestry of Pripyat's past. Together, they walked the streets of her youth. They watched the sun set and reminisced all night until they could watch it rise again.

During the following day, the lovers sat on a low bucket on the Ferris wheel. The sounds of children echoed around the amusement park as families gathered. Someone approached with an announcement. The entire time, Alex and Katya never let go of one another.

When the light faded from Chernobyl, the painting came to an end, silently disappearing back into memory. Stillness filled the air—a silence that was finally broken by the sounds of birds cawing in the forest.

The woodsman stepped out of his cabin to meet a pack of animals that had gathered to play. In the village, ovens were lit and breakfast was made before the gardens were tended. Life in the dream continued.

One thing remained. The roses planted in Pripyat began to bloom brightly, more magnificently than ever before.

While the villagers had never felt the compulsion to enter the city except for the festival, the crimson glow of the flowers caught their attention and lured them closer. They would occasionally picnic in the city, when the weather was nice. Sometimes they simply took walks through town to admire the sights. The gardeners helped maintain the roses year-round to preserve their beauty.

The following year, the Festival of Lights was more vibrant than ever. With Pripyat properly resembling a city of roses, a new theme of love and companionship naturally entered the celebration. The villagers were happy. The dream would never end.

On the last day of the festival that year, a lone berehynia sat on the Ferris wheel, holding a rose in its hands. It quietly listened, bobbing its head from side to side until it heard the laughter of a couple enjoying their time together.

Flying to the bucket of the Ferris wheel where the sound originated, the berehynia left the rose on the seat in memoriam. Smiling, it fluttered away, leaving them together in peace and forever in love.

The end.

About the Author

Donovan Pruitt has a passion for science fiction and fantasy, especially those titles that trend toward young and new adult storytelling. *City of Roses* is his first standalone book as an indie author, though he has also written for video games and was previously published as a co-author in the fantasy genre. You can visit him online at www.KalaEmpire.com or join the discussion on Twitter @KalaEmpire.